To Margaret
lovely sense
& care for the

Freddy Anderson -
March 1992

A read at the few
leisure times in your busy life.

C000121463

Oiney Hoy

Oiney Hoy

a satirical, Irish novel

Freddy Anderson

Polygon
EDINBURGH

© Freddy Anderson 1989
Polygon
22 George Square, Edinburgh

Set in Linotron Sabon by
Polyprint, Edinburgh and
printed and bound in Great Britain by
Redwood Burn Limited, Trowbridge, Wiltshire

British Library Cataloguing in
Publication Data
Anderson, Freddy
Oiney Hoy.
I. Title
823'.914 [F]

ISBN 0 7486 6034 8

To my staunch Scottish comrade of Mayo descent Isobel Foy, and our three children, Paul, Isobel Rae and Dermot.

Acknowledgements

To John Ferguson, recently deceased, a gentle, generous soul, a rare gem who helped not only this book but my broader view of Mankind. To historian Dr James Young of Stirling University and author James Kelman, both of whom gave me valuable assistance. To the Scottish poet and folklore researcher Dr Hamish Henderson, my cherished friend since 1946. Last and not least to Jenny Turner and Polygon, who made excellent suggestions to assist greatly in the final version of Oiney's wanderings.

Oiney Hoy

This is the story of a boy with a nickname that he did not like one wee bit until one strange day when he met a bold fellow by the name of Shaun at a Wake. Oiney Hoy was the boy's sobriquet in his native village, Creevan, in the very heart of Ireland. I was about to call it a God-forsaken wee place, but that would be a lie. Nature endowed Creevan, which is the Gaelic word for twig or little branch, with two lovely lakes surrounded by frail reeds and three small hills, one of which, with its mantle of bluebells and green ferns reflected in the still waters, is like a vision of fairyland.

No! Creevan was not forsaken by God or Nature, but by the rich landowners of Ireland, so that for centuries the poor had to leave home and search for work in foreign lands. Oiney Hoy's grandmother, however, was able to remain in Creevan, where she sold apples and oranges and bananas. She had a fruit stall in the Market Square, and woe betide you if you passed without buying some of her goods. She would hurl sharp stinging invective after your retreating figure and even lambast your poor dead ancestors. It was a tongue like hers put the curse on Cromwell that his warts would bleed venom and a restored monarch dance on his grave. On the three braes of Creevan she was known to every man, woman and child as 'The Holy Terror'.

The original Oweney Hoy, pronounced 'Oiney Hoy' in Creevan, was a poor, old amadhaun, or green fool, of the Carrick Hills to the south of the village. A tall, thin, bony man, like Don Quixote, and strange enough in his own way, he lived about a hundred years ago in a tumbledown, thatched shed on a bleak hillside. Of his many eccentric deeds, one is especially remembered for its quaintness in that remote countryside. Oiney spread the word around the Carrick Hills that, on a coming Sunday, he was going to die for Ireland. The event, he said, would take place in the Long Meadow below the chapel after second Mass. At first the wise old folk shook their heads from side to side, and said, 'How in God's name can he die for Ireland when there's not an empty gallows or a redcoat around for miles?' The antics of the poor fool, however, drew a score or two to the Long Meadow that Sunday. There they saw Oiney, stripped to the waist and standing about fifty yards to the side of a cutting filled to near the brim with black bogwater. In a few minutes he was turning his wild sky-blue eyes to the gawking spectators: 'You all forget the men o' '98, an' the bold Fenian men, for the priests don't tell you everythin', do they?' he shouted.

'What about the Famine, Oiney?' cried a smart young wag as he ran to hide behind a bank of turf. 'Do you remember that, Oiney?'

'Oiney remembers the lot! God bless Wolfe Tone an' Napper Tandy!'

Then he blessed himself three times and wearing no shoes or stockings made a mad run for the bog-hole. A mighty cheer arose from the astonished crowd when Oiney took off in a great leap. Some of them even blessed themselves. The folk of the Carrick Hills were as fervent devotees of sport as religion but they had never seen such a jump. The cheers of delight continued, but in the midst of the happy host, poor Oiney looked lost and bewildered. Then the priest came down from the chapel gates and, lifting his clothes and shoes, led the sad hero out onto the road, back to his lonely hillside shack.

A few years later Oiney died, but his leap and his strange antics became a rich memory around the turf-fires of many a home in Carrick on a cold winter's night. I remember hearing these tales when, as a boy of seven, I lay in the wooden box-bed in my aunt's kitchen watching the peat flames send the shadows flickering across the rafters high in the hills. 'Oiney's Lepp', as it was called locally, became a well-known landmark, like the priests' Mass Rock from the Penal Days. Then a peculiar thing happened. As each generation cut more peat, the famous bog-hole in the Long Meadow extended and Oiney's feat became more amazing. Wide-eyed school-children would stare in wonder at the great feat of their antecedent. Even the scholarly folklorists up at Trinity College in Dublin took a lively interest in the phenomenon when 'Oiney's Lepp' extended the whole length of the Long Meadow to become a superhuman marvel, rivalling the great, magic wonders of Finn and Cuchulainn. Its growing importance can be illustrated by the fact that Oiney's Lepp became the subject of a three-inch footnote in Professor Seagull's great work, *An Oral History of Our Time* (The Chapter 8: Legend becomes Myth).

Oiney's strange character survived as well, and in a somewhat similar manner. With the growth of a small-scale industry in the neighbouring villages and towns quite a number of the Carrick hill-folk descended into Creevan and became residents there. They seldom forgot their origins, however. When, for example, a trembling offspring of theirs wet the school floor on examination for First Communion or some such innocent mishap, a Creevan mother would exclaim in anger, 'Shamin' your dacint mother an' father is it? Makin' wather on the Master's clane floor! My God, but you're every bit as daft as Oiney Hoy.'

It was only with the Holy Terror's grandson, however, that the name really stuck. A tall, rather slim, gangly lad with large, innocent blue eyes, red hair and hundreds of freckles, his small mouth was ever agape in amazement at the strange world in which he found himself walking. The name clung to him like his large jutting ears and ran after him as well, playing tig with his own shadow on the summer streets of Creevan. And indeed, by a very strange metempsychosis, some of the quaint spirit of the poor, green fool of the Carrick Hills took possession of him. This quite naturally annoyed his granny who was always complaining that already there were more than enough fools in the world. It was just that he was never out of trouble.

The first time was when he was seven years old. She had bought him an emerald green jersey which was meant to serve a double purpose – his First Communion and the Hibernian Rally to the town of Cavan. The latter event was always a great day of glory for her. She carried a magnificent green banner with a golden harp embroidered on it on these occasions, joining the bands as they marched through the street playing 'The Harp That Once Through Tara's Halls' and 'Let Erin Remember'. God bless Tommy Moore, she would say to herself. He knew the words and tunes to make the heart glow. Me harp as well he's talking about. Me harp that once through Cavan streets its soul of music shed. She did not understand deeply the politics of it all but she had a great picture of the Irish martyr-hero, Robert Emmet, over the mantelpiece in the kitchen. She had no love for Orangemen. She thought them as much Irish as the Eskimos of the frozen north or the poor aborigines of the Bush.

The boy with the emerald jersey joined three of his pals to explore one of the lakes beside Creevan. There was a secret labyrinth known only to them which ran past the swans' nest among the golden reeds. A large white upturned enamel bath had drifted in near the shore. It had probably been discarded by the local Protestant minister who wore grey spats, or by some other well-to-do; poor Catholics had only coarse zinc ones. The delighted boys hauled their find into the reeds. They filled the plug-hole and a smaller, rusty-edged opening with a yellow putty-like clay from the bank. From the long fresh rushes on the lakeside they wove lengths to attach to the bath through the tap-hole. Certain now that they were the owners of a seaworthy vessel, they unanimously elected Oiney to be the gallant skipper of the mighty craft on its trial run.

'Heave ho, me hearties,' they shouted. 'All aboard!' Even though, with the exception of Oiney, all of them were safely ashore.

They pushed the bath clear of the reeds into the fresh-water lake under a burning sun. The snow-white swans floated gracefully beside their nest, eyeing the boy and his crazy boat suspiciously; he was aware that if aroused they could give a powerful blow with their wings. The young mariner, however, was too elated by his adventure to worry about wind, weather or waterfowl. Then, quite suddenly, dramatically, the yellow clay putty began to dissolve and shift. His short pants became soaking wet; the bath sank under him and he was left floundering and splashing in the water. His pals hauled him ashore. Soaked to the skin, he stood shivering on the hillside, not so much from the cold water but from fear of the Holy Terror: 'Oh God, she'll murdher me!' he cried. 'As soon as she lays hands on me, she'll murdher me. Oh, me good new green gansey. Would you look at it?'

'Naw, naw,' said one of the boys. 'We'll dry you out on the hill here an' she doesn't need to know a thing about it.'

He sat naked on the grass, while his friends made a close circle around him to hide him from view and keep the news of his shipwreck from the ears of his granny. Soon his clothes dried out in that hot July sky over Ireland, and all seemed to be going well. He dressed himself hurriedly, and then looking down at his clothes, groaned in dismay. 'Oh, holy God, would you look at me new gansey!'

The boys all stared in amazement. The green jersey had shrunk six inches in the drying process. 'Me arms were never that long,' cried poor Oiney. 'I can never go home to her like this.'

One of the boys had a brainwave: 'I know what,' he shouted triumphantly. 'You can tell her you just grew out of it. That's it. You had these growin' pains. Our Maisie had them. That solves it.'

An hour later the boys huddled near the door as their pal went in to face his irate granny. 'Ah, Jaysus, Mary an' Joseph,' she wailed, 'what have you done with your lovely gansey that I bought you for the big rally in Cavan on Sunday an' your Holy Communion as well, you rapscallion of a tinker's get, that brings your poor granny woe an' worry. Ah, mother o' God, would you just look at the gapin', gawkin' open mouth o' the eejit! I declare to the Almighty you're every bit as daft an' worse than Oiney Hoy, the great amadhaun of the Carrick Hills.'

5

The boys, chuckling with glee, crept away from the door to tell the village of the misadventure and how the Holy Terror had called her grandson all those terrible names, one name in particular that set Creevan laughing until sunset. Memories of the poor fool of the hills floated over the rooftops, hovering between the chapel spire and the three braes, and in the kitchens and snugs of the little village, where superstition and gossip often ousted common sense, a new Oiney Hoy was born in the very heart of Ireland.

The Circuit Judge

It was on a Sunday morning that the Gunner Reagan from Arva arrived in Creevan with his poor wife and young family. He called himself the gunner because he had served in the British Army in that capacity in World War I, and was forever boasting of his great deeds in the trenches. After installing his family in a shabby little house in the Lane where the sun seldom shone, he went into Doyle's public-house by way of the back-yard. This Doyle had a bad reputation. His brother had been shot as an Informer during the Black-and-Tan War in Ireland and more recently the publican had barred an unfrocked priest.

What made Doyle really despised was that he took the priest's money and let him drink like a fish before he was unfrocked. And he had the nerve to pretend that he was only doing it for the clergyman's own good. The unfrocked priest did not take the insult lightly. Folk said that he was seen to stand outside Doyle's closed door at the dead of night with his stole around his shoulders and his right hand raised in a mighty curse. This curse ended with the terrible words, 'May the green grass grow over your doorstep for lack of customers!' People in Creevan swear to this day that for several years this came to pass, but then there are people in Creevan who will swear to anything. The poet Yeats would have reaped a richer harvest of fairy lore in Creevan than beyond in the country lanes of Sligo.

On that same Sunday that the Gunner Reagan from Arva drank his way through the last Mass, the Holy Terror was sitting on a stool at the door of her cottage. She was saying her rosary beads out loud as she gazed across the street at the pious chapelgoers on their way up the brae;

she knew every mother's son of them and their cousins in America.

Oiney stood in the shadows of the small stone-flagged kitchen, wondering what he would do to pass the time. Winter in Creevan was a long weary season, little relieved by Hallowe'en and Christmas. The old woman became even more irksome during that period; she showed scarcely any festive goodwill or charity towards her neighbours or Oiney. He listened to her mumblings at the door until they became audible to him. Her voice was now raised a good deal louder as though she wanted the chapelgoers to hear her lambast them. Good God, thought the boy, what a strange prayer she was saying! If there was an Almighty up there in Heaven, He would surely strike her stone dead.

The rosary beads, polished and worn, slid through her wrinkled fingers. 'Hail Mary, full o' Grace,' she prayed, 'would you look at the bloody conceit of their sanctified faces! Full o' Grace be damned! I mind the day when the lot o' them came down from Carrick into Creevan without as much as an arse, God forgive me, to their trousers . . . The Lord is with Thee and blessed is the fruit o' Thy womb – Jesus! . . . Ah, Jesus, haven't the snotty-nosed gets risen up in the world . . . Minnie Downey beyond hadn't the dacint shift to her back . . . By the crucified Jesus look at her now an' the halo chokin' her . . . Holy Mary, mother o' God, pray for us sinners . . . Sinners an' damn blackguards if you ask me . . . Now and at the hour of our death. Amen.'

This prayer sounded quite a bit different from the ones he was taught in the school on the hill. The school however had its own strangeness. Oiney did not learn very much in it except the Catechism and how to write at an angle of forty-five degrees in a copybook. A few other things also. He learned that Ireland was an island set in the Atlantic, that God made the world more like an orange than a ball, flat on top, that an imaginary line ran around the middle of it called the Equator. Even more important still, he learned that he was the proud possessor of a thing called a Soul.

Now this Soul, he was taught, was invisible, odourless, and colourless, and his greatest task on Earth was to save this Soul so that it would meet other invisible, odourless and colourless Souls of its kind in an invisible world called Heaven. Oiney was taught this by the priest and the schoolteacher without as much as a wink or a wicked grin on their faces, so young Oiney accepted it as gospel truth. If by chance he did not save this precious soul of his the threat hung over him that he would cruelly burn in the snake-pits of Hell for all eternity. Faced with such a dreadful alternative, everything but the saving of his soul shrank into insignificance. Believing his elders and his teachers, for they seemed to entertain no doubts on the subject, he was prepared to believe almost anything. Illusion and reality had lost their dividing line for him; his mouth opened a little wider and he became even more gullible.

It was late that Sunday night when the Gunner Reagan emerged from Doyle's public-house and awakened Creevan with his loud bawling. 'You want to know who and what I am, do you? Well, I'll tell you. I'm the Gunner Reagan from Arva. That's what I am. I'm a Cavan Slasher an' I'll knock you all into the middle o' next week. I'll have you for me breakfast an' I'll bate the best man in the country of Ireland.' He stumbled over to the village pump at the top of the Market House brae. This cast iron fountain was moulded into the shape of a lion's head with an English constable's peaked helmet on top of it, a relic of Imperial rule.

The Gunner threw his arms around the pump. 'Hello, Sergeant,' he said in a slurred voice. 'Were you out on your own patrolling the streets of this one-horse town? Fare thee well, Enniskillen, we'll return in full bloom. You and me, Sergeant, for a square-go! Eh? What's about it? It'll warm the two of us up . . .'

He hit the cast iron pump a whack with his fist and then quickly recoiled with the shock. 'Aw, Jaysus,' he cried with the pain, 'but you're the hard, hard man. It's a cruel world altogether an' me a wanderer in me own land.' And then through the heavy, sodden fog created in his mind by the long day in Doyle's pub, there appeared in a sudden flicker of remembrance the faces of his wife and children and he awkwardly stumbled down the dark narrow Lane where the poor folk lived. The blustering bellowing died away and Creevan, with a sigh of relief, went to sleep.

The following day, Monday, was the eve of the Circuit Court Session, when the crusty, pompous Judge Ritchie and his servile minions presided over the trials. The old Court House lay at the foot of the Market House brae; it was a low, long, sandstone building with two Ionic columns, and a massive oak door studded with heavy iron nails. Every Court Session the door was left open, for the Judge complained, with some justification, that the place smelled like an Egyptian tomb.

In the evening of that Monday, Oiney was sent by his granny to fetch a bucket of water from the pump. He climbed the Market House brae and set his bucket down under the lion's mouth. Then he turned the serrated handle which was located where the lion's ear should have been. The clear, sparkling water flowed in abundance. It quickly filled the bucket and overflowed onto the brae. Oiney tried desperately to turn it off, but without success; the publican and the local Civic Guard had a go, but they fared no better. The gushing water spread across the street at the fountain head and poured like a stream down the brae. It was as though a mischievous leprechaun in the pump, aroused by Gunner Reagan's fierce thump, had taken over the inner workings and was determined to have revenge for its rude awakening. All evening long the water flowed, and right into the small hours of the morning. Then quite suddenly and mysteriously the flow ceased as if the imp, at last satisfied, had gone to sleep himself. There was a hard frost that morning and, later on, a light fall of snow.

Such was the idyllic picture-postcard scene of an Irish snow-clad village which greeted Judge Ritchie as he took pompous strides from the Market Square towards the Court

House. What a quaint delightful scene, he thought, with the old, uneven houses, the village pump and ancient market-place, an olde worlde scene that he hoped would endure, like his prestige, forever. And then suddenly it happened. Some say that the malevolent leprechaun in the fountain drew him towards the spot where the treacherous ice began. Others stubbornly insist that the Judge acted spontaneously, of his own volition, and should not be denied the credit of an astonishing performance.

Suffice it to say that somewhere in the vicinity of the pump the learned Judge took off, not in any legal or judicial sense, but literally took off in a physical, corporeal manner. In short, he left terra firma. If he had gone into orbit the villagers of Creevan could not have been more astonished. Wide-eyed with wonder, they gazed at an aspect of the stern law-dispenser they had never known existed. Admittedly the first sudden jerk for an instant caused some splay-footed panic in an attempt to regain his dignified stride, but by a magnificent effort of sheer will-power he drew both legs together, and with the calm composure we have come to expect from the Law, briefcase firmly clasped, bowler-hatted, brolly over left arm, he slid down the steep brae, as gracefully as any Markova.

The widow Murtagh, who lived about twenty yards down from the fountain, had this to say to reporters:

'An outstanding performance! I was doing me washin' an' lookin' over me half-door when His Worship passed. His face looked a kind of frozen stiff, but then it always does. But polite, always meticulous polite. "Good-day, your honour," I said, "A nice day for ducks." "Good-day, madam," he said, raising his bowler. Did I notice anything particular about his feet? Well, they did seem a bit glued together an' he was slidin' in a kind o' pollyglide. But I'm not versed in these modern dances.'

It was the Judge's amazing antics halfway down the brae which astonished the youth of Creevan, who foolishly imagined they were rare performers on the ice. They soon realised that, compared to the Judge, they were second-rate amateurs. First he enacted a series of hunker slides, flailing his legs from side to side like a Cossack dancer; then he performed several back-benders, arching his body like a dolphin; then a tremendous somersault, clinging unsuccessfully to his brolly and briefcase, while the boys cheered his generosity every bit as much as his prowess. Stern-faced and stony-hearted as he was generally, on this occasion he showed a generosity of spirit that was very touching.

One has only to hear poor Mrs Doyle's glowing report.

'I was standin' at me door when His Honour passed. Maybe then he was only about three feet off the ground an' doin' these crazy loop-the-loop things. I told him it wasn't right for a man of his age, to be doin' cartwheels an' the like ... But he didn't answer, just threw his umbrella at me ... God knows I'm grateful, most grateful for it. If I get a soakin' wet, I do get these awful pains in me joints ... Ah, God bless him, His Honour was in a charitable mood that day, for Tim Ryan, the saddler, whose son got six months from His Nibs at the last Assizes, received the good leather briefcase. I suppose it was his way of atonin' for the heavy sentence ... An' even the boys o' Creevan benefitted that day by his tumblin' generosity. He scattered silver an' copper coins all over the brae. They say, though, that he gave shockin' sentences after he sailed into Court through the open door that day ... aye sailed ... over the benches an' into his seat. And believe me, it was all the fault of that rapscallion of a boy, Oiney Hoy, who turned the pump on. For years afterwards we had many's the good laugh about it, an' we all thought for ages in Creevan that a Circuit Judge was one of them puffed up Law Lords who perform cartwheels and somersaults on the ice on their way to Court.'

On Erin's Green Valleys

It was several years later. Winter was past and the bright days of spring shone on Erin's green valleys. Saint Patrick's Day was only a week away when the Holy Terror sent Oiney along the ditch to find shamrocks on the road to Cootehill, that same little flat town in the north of Cavan where some villains had murdered Nell Flaherty's drake. Near the old Boiler House at the crossroads, where the Quakers made the controversial soup in the Famine times, the young lad met Terry Doogan of the Hills, driving an ass and cart into Creevan. He was quite a tall man, with a slight stoop and a glossy brown beard; he spoke poetry and riddles with a loud deep voice. He often broke off in his conversation to recite a line or two from one of the patriotic ballads of Ireland.

'Is it true, Terry,' Oiney asked innocently, 'that you don't go to chapel?'

Terry paused for a minute. 'As true, God bless us,' he said, 'as the cross on that ass's back, and it got that cross implanted as a token of favour for carryin' Christ from the wilderness into Jerusalem on Palm Sunday. "Into our town-land on a night o'snow rode a man from God knows where . . ." And that's a fact.'

'Why don't you go, Terry?' Oiney persisted.

'Ah, sure God himself only knows. Maybe it's the lingerin' smell o' the incense or the pungent smoke o' the snuffed candles, but a great sickness comes over me when I cross the chapel door, a terrible nausea indeed, and I seem to be trapped in the temples o' the ancients. But sure "my cathedral is the glory of the skies, the heat of noon or the first sun-rise . . ." I'm on me way, son, but good luck to you in your search!'

A little bit further up the road Oiney met a lean, dark young man in a trenchcoat and a hat tilted low over his brow. 'You are from Creevan?'

'I am,' said Oiney.

'Tell me something!'

'Tell you something? If I can.'

'About Doyle the publican in the Market Square. Is he dead yet?'

'No,' said Oiney, 'but he's got the Last Rites an' they've taken him to Monaghan hospital.'

The lean man chuckled.

'The Last Rites, did you say? Good.'

'Why?' asked Oiney, a little puzzled by the stranger's glee.

'Why? Ah, why? That's the question you might say. Well now ... I see ... Won't it be a great comfort to his crossin' the unknown boundaries o' the Great Divide?'

The man took his leave, but in days ahead Oiney had cause to remember that strange encounter.

In searching the ditch for shamrocks, to his delight, he found not only many sprigs of the famous plant but down in the deep grass a shining half-crown and a penny piece. His granny steeped the shamrocks in water and let him keep the penny. 'We'll send the half-crown to the Missions,' she said, 'an' buy a black baby. And if you're good, I'll take you on the pilgrimage to Lough Derg...'

'Lough Derg, granny? What's Lough Derg?'

'It's an island.'

Oiney looked puzzled.

'An island? I thought you said it was a lough.'

'My God, didn't they learn you anything at all at that school on the hill? There's a holy island on Lough Derg, where the great Saint Patrick himself, Apostle of Ireland, prayed and fasted in a dark cave for forty days an' forty nights...'

'What did he do that for?'

She gave her grandson a look of great scorn and then

mimicked his voice. 'What did he do that for? What did he do that for? Wasn't he lookin' for paper to wipe his arse with? What did he do that for! Wasn't he prayin' for the conversion of the Irish, you, you amadhuan. An' God answered his prayer except for them bloody Orange crew up north . . . God revealed Himself to Patrick.'

'He did what?' said the open-mouthed Oiney.

'Shut your gob or you'll be catchin' flies, gasson! God appeared to Patrick in a spinning white light. He told the saint that on a dark day ahead the lovely green valleys of Erin would slowly sink undher the waves o' the Atlantic. An' that Patrick himself would have the privilege o' sittin' in judgement on the Irish race!'

'He did not!'

'He did or else I wouldn't be tellin' you! Why else would the great pilgrimages to Lough Derg in Donegal be made for throughout the centuries? Prayin' an' fastin' an' sayin' the Stations in our bare feet. Three days an' nights with nothin' but a crust o' bread an' black tay an' the flint cuttin' your feet an' you chitterin' with the cold, with the bitther winds from the wild Atlantic crossin' the bleak, bare hills o' Donegal . . .'

It sounded so dreadfully forlorn and incredibly weird that Oiney, bored by the long winter in Creevan, felt a great desire to visit the strange place. So, for some weeks, he kept close to the house and ran the messages. He fetched buckets of water from the familiar old lion-headed fountain on the brae, and scoured all the little bottles which ailing neighbours sent in to his granny for a taste of the cure, when it came, from the holy island. One bottle in particular which his granny warned him to rinse well with lashings of soap and water and elbow grease was an empty whiskey bottle sent in by old Terry of the Hills, who she said, God forgive him, never crossed a chapel door. 'Scour it well,' she ordered the boy, 'for the evil dregs o' whiskey will polluther the holy wather somethin' awful, an' instead of a cure cause a calamity.'

One morning in June, the slow train drew the Lough Derg pilgrims westwards to Donegal . . . Oiney, carrying a well-rinsed and scrubbed lemonade bottle, sat beside his granny and eyed the others in the carriage. Like the old woman, many were saying their rosary beads, while others dreamed as they looked out of the windows at the grazing cattle in the lovely, patchwork of green and corn-gold fields of Ulster, in by Fermanagh where 'the Erne shall run red with redundance of blood, the earth shall rock beneath our tread . . . ere you shall fade, ere you shall die, my dark Rosaleen . . .'

Oiney, with his own innate kindness and love for his people, gazed innocently into the eyes of the other pilgrims and saw not sin nor selfishness, but instead a little bit too much humility, he thought, and the strain of overwork and worry. These were not the brash sinners that the brimstone missionaries should thunder at from the pulpits raised high above the poor. There was scarcely a soul among them knew what real sin was. These were people more sinned against than sinning, but still afraid of the loss of their invisible souls, as Oiney was afraid.

'Tickets, please!' The powerful voice of the Inspector boomed along the corridor so loudly that Oiney was amazed to discover that its possessor was in fact quite a small man in uniform, crowned by a shiny peak cap. Just then a sharp elbow dug into the boy's ribs, and he heard his granny whisper in alarm, 'Pull your trousers above your knees, gasson! Quick!'

Oiney could scarcely believe her command. 'What, granny?'

'D'you as you're bid,' she shouted frantically, 'for I only got you a half-fare ticket! For Jaysus sake, hurry!'

Oiney's face went scarlet to match his hair almost and he fumbled in embarrassment with the empty lemonade bottle, passing it from one hand to the other. Before he had time to make his mind up what to do, the ticket Inspector stood in their section of the carriage. The old woman, now the picture of piety, handed him the two tickets. He punched one of them and then looked at the other over and over again. Lifting his eyes from the ticket, he looked at Oiney, measuring him up, then back to the ticket again and finally at the empty lemonade bottle, as though it played some mysterious role in all this. 'What age are you, son?'

The old woman was ready to pounce on him. 'Is there anyone askin' you your age, is there?'

The wee man stood his full five-feet-two-inches tall, officialdom triumphant. 'I would like to inform you, madam, that I am an Inspector of the Great Northern Railway.'

'I don't give a damn if you own the Great Northern Railway. Fetch me a real Inspector that respects people's rights, an' us pious pilgrims, no less, doin' penance on the way to the holy Lough Derg!'

The other passengers had their faces turned to the windows, desperately striving to show that they had no connection whatsoever with this awful woman. But the Holy Terror had had so many sharp rebuffs in life that she shrugged off this latest one. 'What are you anyway, you impudent get,' she snapped at the official, 'that you come bursting in on top of me rosary beads? Are you a haythen heretic or worse still a bitther Orangeman that you disturb the peace of a Christian carriage? Have I asked you what religion you are or what you had for your breakfast? If you don't go this minit, I've a mind to summon you before the Stipendiary.' She had a liking for these nineteenth-century words; they sounded so important they frightened people off.

The Inspector, realising that he had an impossible case on his hands, thought it wiser to make a safe retreat, but he fired a parting salvo.

'You can be up for defraudin' the Great Northern Railway . . .'

She was on her feet again. 'If you don't lave me sight this instant the Great Northern Railway will be minus an Inspector before we reach the next station! We hanged a wee fella like you in Carrick during the Land War!'

For the remainder of the journey Oiney could not say that he enjoyed the ensuing peace. His granny's tongue rattled away at a great rate. The entire carriage-full of penitents seemed to be staring at his hot, blushing face, making him feel guilty of the terrible crime of belonging to the scourge of Creevan.

This was only the beginning of his penance. From the small jetty at the lough-side, they could see the lone bleak island with its basilica, guest house and other buildings. For well over a thousand years, pilgrims from Ireland, Scotland, England and the Continent had stood on these ancient shores. Soon a medium-sized ferryboat was carrying them across the waves to be welcomed on the island pier by Dean Keown. Oiney saw the Dean give his granny a very strange look, for he knew her well, and probably anticipated a rough time of it.

It was not long before the old woman and the boy began their rounds of the Stations – or beds, as they were called. There were several of these bleak, stony circles, and the barefoot route of the pilgrims lay across sharp-edged flintstone. Oiney picked his pious way very gingerly, but his granny made ample atonement for his avoidance of pain by falling on top of him at regular intervals and accompanying these falls with loud shrieks of 'Oh, Christ, me corns,' 'Oh, Jesus, me bunions'. For Oiney it was like two or three extra penances, and no one on that island was so glad to see the ferryboat arrive to take them all back to the mainland. Dean Keown saw them off and once again Oiney noticed that peculiar look in the priest's eyes as he made sure the boy's granny was safely on board. Dean Keown seemed to give vent to a great sigh of heartfelt relief.

It was a different ticket Inspector on the train home and for a considerable time nothing disturbed the peace and contentment. After the long spells of vigil on Lough Derg, most of the pilgrims fell asleep. Oiney's exhausted grandmother lay back, snoring quite loudly, while the lad counted the passing telegraph poles. Then, for no apparent reason, he suddenly became conscious of the lemonade bottle in his hand. For days he had been carrying it from place to place almost unaware of its very existence. Now he sat stunned, looking at its emptiness. In the midst of the confusion and anxiety on Lough Derg, he had forgotten to fill the bottle with holy water. Nor had his granny noticed the empty bottle either.

He sat for quite a while, really dismayed by the awful discovery. Terry of the Hills, the Widow Murtagh, Mrs Coyle, and the other poor suffering neighbours would be bitterly disappointed. Oiney had brought no holy water home to pour into the little miniature bottles. It was surely bad enough, he thought, to deprive his poor neighbours of a cure for their pains. But to have to hold up his empty bottle and to look in their sad eyes was more than he could bear.

Then suddenly, he had a flash of inspiration, a flash of genius. It was not the fault of the leprechaun of the fountain this time, but the train happened to be passing through the territory of smugglers and the like just then, and who knows but Old Nick himself had a hand in it?

Now ordinary water is the same as holy water as far as the layman is concerned anyhow. It has the same transparent colour and the same consistency. So thought Oiney, in this emergency, only in this emergency, if Terry of the Hills and the others get their miniatures filled with ordinary water, they will not be any the wiser. Of course, reasoned Oiney, ordinary water will effect no cure, but then even the best holy water from Lourdes in France will not always produce a cure. And thus the poor sufferers will not blame Oiney. It was deception, downright deception indeed, but in a worthy cause, and as the Jesuit sophists might say, the end justifying the means.

His granny, thank heavens, was still asleep, and the rest of the pilgrims resting back on clear consciences, when Oiney crept forward along the corridor. No one present, had they looked, would have dreamed in a million years that this small, freckled, pious and innocent boy had an empty bottle stuck up his jersey. He sneaked quietly into the toilet, snibbed the door behind him and filled the bottle with good clear train water from the sink tap.

Old Terry of the Hills, the Widow Murtagh and Mrs Coyle were highly delighted, as were all the others. Oiney stood, blushing with guilt, as they expressed their warm thanks. They mistook his blushes for shyness. A week later his embarrassment was even greater when they came from all parts to thank his granny for the powerful 'cure' she had brought them. 'Thanks be to God an' His holy Mother,' said Mrs Murtagh, 'for I've never felt as good in a month o' Sundays. Me spots have disappeared an' not only that, but me daughter, Peggy, is coughin' betther.' She patted Oiney on the head and never even noticed that his freckles had disappeared in a huge crimson blush.

'Bless his wee soul,' she added fervently, 'but who knows he's got the makin's of a holy Bishop in him yet.'

Oiney nurtured silently his terrible sin until the autumn when the missionaries roared into Creevan. Previously he had been afraid to tell his heinous sin in Confession in case the priest recognised him. There were few local lads who had ever been to Lough Derg. At least the missionaries for all their sulphur and brimstone carried your sins back to Dublin with them and well clear of the Parish. Waiting until the queue was clear, Oiney went into Confession: 'Bless me Father for I have sinned.'

'How long is it since your last Confession?'

'It must be three or four months, Father.'

'That's a long time for a lad like you. Well now, let's have your sins!'

'Well, Father, it's like this. I went to Lough Derg, but I didn't take home any holy water at all. I took train-water.'

'Drain-water,' said the priest, who was hard of hearing. 'Tell me more about this drain-water! Were you digging drains in Donegal?'

'No, Father, it wasn't drain-water; it was train-water.'

'Oh, I see. Rain-water. I see. But tell me, how did you take home rain-water from Lough Derg?'

'Father,' said Oiney, almost giving up hope, 'I filled the bottle full of water from the sink tap in the train.'

The missionary tried to get a glimpse of this strange penitent. 'And what in God's name did you do that for?'

'I pretended it was holy water, Father.'

'But sure,' said the priest, 'that kind of water wouldn't cure.'

'But it did, Father, it did,' cried Oiney almost triumphantly. 'It cured Peggy's cough, an' her Ma's spots an' Mrs Coyle . . .'

'Were you tempting God?' the priest asked suspiciously.

'Oh no, Father, shure I wouldn't endanger my invisible soul,' Oiney assured him.

Quaint fellow this, thought the priest, but basically harmless. 'Say the Stations of the Cross as a penance! And don't put drain-water, or train-water or whatever in holy water bottles again!'

'But Father?'

'What is it now?' said the priest impatiently.

'Father? How did the water cure them when it wasn't holy? How did it do that, Father?'

'Listen, young man, and take my word for it. Sure all the water in Ireland is holy!'

The Belfry

The belfry, high up in the spire of St Patrick's Church in Creevan, was a real vantage point for a grand view of the surrounding countryside. From it you could see the Carrick Hills and the twin loughs and the little historic roads winding their way down towards the ford and village. Jonjo Cooney, its sexton, was a mere mortal on the Creevan streets, but up here in the belfry, he was monarch of all he surveyed. He felt aloof and superior, looking down like a god on all the little moving dots that comprised the local residents.

He could watch, for example, 'Springheel Willie', his conceited old master, stride with that peculiar bounce on his way to the school on the hill. He could see the Civic Guard sergeant, nicknamed 'Pat Oats' after the famous porridge, loiter with intent near one or other of the public houses. On the other side of the street he could see Father Duffy, the parish priest, move to and fro among his flock, a busy beetle indeed, while Susan Cairns, that shrill soprano in the chapel choir, now seemed a mere, little ladybird insect by her garden pond.

No wonder, thought Jonjo, God feels such power and might, gazing as He does down on the world from the immense heights of the Universe. Jonjo, like Oiney, was a strange enough fellow himself who found it very difficult and sad to grow up into an ordinary dull citizen of the world. He retained a fondness for the games and hobbies of children, such as collecting cigarette cards and playing marbles. On the Castle Hill, he often flew kites. As a chapel sexton, he could no longer rob orchards, of course, but he often kept a look-out on 'Pat Oats' for Oiney and the other boys. He would always be a youngster at heart.

Peering down from the belfry window, he now saw his friend, Oiney, climb the rows of stone steps up towards the chapel door. He recognised quite easily Oiney's peculiar skip-and-jump and soon the sexton's face wore a smile as he welcomed his friend into his little kingdom on high. There were few others in Creevan had accesss to that lofty eyrie of Jonjo's. 'Good man yourself, Oiney, you're just in time.' He pointed out the Monaghan road and a far distance beyond Tullycorbet, where a small black speck could be seen moving slowly.

'That's the hearse, Oiney, takin' the publican, Doyle, back to the big shop in the Square. Tell me when he comes to Dr Nolan's house below there an' I'll start ringing the bell for the dead.'

'All right, Jonjo,' said Oiney, throwing himself down on a small bale of straw close to the window. 'I'm your man.'

'What did you learn about Lough Derg, Oiney?'

'Oh, I wouldn't go there again, Jonjo, without a fur coat. An' definitely, no granny. She's out ... But d'you know what I heard the ferrymen talk about on the way back? There was a bit of a storm on Lough Derg, but they were sayin' it was nothin' to the terrible year of 1795 ... the 12th of July 1795 when a boat o' pilgrims sank with all hands aboard ...'

'God bless us an' save us,' said Jonjo, aghast with the news, however belated, 'but wouldn't they go straight to Heaven ...? A bit o' consolation indeed for their bereaved relatives. The 12th of July did you say? Maybe them Orangemen spiked the boat. You see, Oiney, that was the time Orangism was startin' up, a whole century, mind you, after King Billy ... They never bothered with King Billy until a hundred years after he was dead and buried.'

'Why was that, Jonjo?'

'Well, Catholic an' Protestant was joinin' together in the United Irishmen. So the British started the Orange Order to keep Ireland divided ...'

'The dirty pigs,' exclaimed Oiney. 'Me granny doesn't like them either.'

'Imagine,' exclaimed Jonjo in a sad but angry voice, 'all them poor souls lost when the Orangemen spiked the boat on Lough Derg! Oiney?'

'What is it, Jonjo?'

'Are you keepin' a good look-out on the road for the hearse?'

'I am, surely.'

'Where is it now?'

'It's just this side of Tullycorbet, Jonjo. Tell me, Jonjo, is Ireland really goin' to sink in the Atlantic five years before the end of the world?'

'Who told you that oul' codswallop, Oiney?' said the startled sexton.

'Me granny said that God told it to Saint Patrick in a cave!'

'In a cave begod,' exclaimed Jonjo with a laugh. 'No wonder He told him it in a cave, for God knows there's a hollow ring to that story, Oiney. You're a bigger cod than Doyle in his coffin, listenin' to your granny's blethers.'

'Tell me, Jonjo! What like was Doyle?'

'What like?'

'Aye. Are you sorry for him an' him dead?'

'Divil the bit. Hadn't he the good innings an' him seventy-two an' more! And he never went without a bite in his purseproud life. Him an' Keenan, the undertaker, were mortal enemies in their great bids to out-do each other.'

'In what way, Jonjo?'

'Well, I'll give you an example. When Keenan bought the paintin' of the Perpetual Supper . . .'

'Succour, Jonjo!'

'Aye, Succour, that's it. I get mixed up at times. When he bought this picture for the chapel Doyle had to go one better, so he bought the big statue of Saint Anthony . . .'

'The one that stands under the organ loft?'

'Aye, Oiney, that's the very one. You're game ball. And then what happened, Oiney? Keenan went an' bought a holy water font for baptisin' the infants. And then lo and behold, Doyle tops that with a set o' bright bronze altar rails . . . and tell me, Oiney, where is he now?'

24

'I suppose,' said Oiney, astonished by all their great gifts to the chapel, 'I suppose, Jonjo, he'll be reapin' his reward in Heaven . . .'

'I didn't mean that at all,' exclaimed Jonjo impatiently. 'I meant where is Doyle's hearse?'

'Oh, the hearse, Jonjo. I thought you meant his soul. The hearse, Jonjo, is at Hanratty's Cross, a wee bit to come still. I suppose the bronze altar rails clinched it for Doyle then?'

'Oh, divil the bit, Oiney, divil the bit. Didn't Keenan up him with a stained-glass window over the High Altar of St Michael oustin' the filthy oul' dragon from Heaven. An' d'you know, Oiney? You'll not believe it.'

'Tell me, Jonjo!'

'D'you know there was the most uncanny resemblance to Doyle on the oul' serpent's face. There was indeed.'

'Begod, Jonjo, they must have hated each other. A stained-glass window no less!'

'They both had the wealth o' Midas an' the pride o' Lucifer in them. They were buyin' their way out o' Purgatory or Hell even, an' at the same time feedin' their conceit . . . They were sittin' on the camel's back an' forcin' it through the needle's eye. But as me mother used to say, Pride comes before a fall. An' she was right.'

'I suppose, Jonjo, the altar rails banjaxed Doyle.'

'If you think that Oiney, you've another guess comin' to you. Indeed an' it didn't. Three months later Doyle disappeared, but when he arrived at Creevan station that August he had a great wooden crate with him . . . He had it brought up on a lorry to the chapel an' opened in front of the parish priest. When the boards were taken asunder, guess what was there, Oiney, guess!'

'I couldn't, Jonjo,' said the excited Oiney. 'I couldn't. You tell me!'

'A great big metal weather-cock to perch on top of the chapel spire. That's what was there Oiney. And you should have seen Doyle's face, beamin' with triumph it was. He turned to Father Duffy an' nudged him, "That gives me somethin' to crow about Father, doesn't it?" An' believe me, Oiney, Keenan was left that day grittin' his teeth.'

Oiney looked out the belfry window. 'Oh, Jonjo, you'll need to hurry with the bell. Doyle's hearse is passin'.'

The slow, ponderous chimes rang out over Creevan. Jonjo then ran over to the straw pile and looked through the window. 'Keenan has the last laugh, Oiney.'

'How, Jonjo?'

The sexton pointed down to the undertaker's shop. 'Look at him standin' there, Oiney, with his legs akimbo as the hearse passes! There he goes raisin' his hat in respect, but I can imagine the grim oul' smirk of satisfaction on his smug face.'

The Wake

From Jonjo's description of the purseproud publican Mr Barney Doyle, Market Square, Creevan, Oiney had not the least desire to attend his Wake and pay respects which certainly, as far as either Jonjo or himself were concerned, did not exist. To him Doyle had always been the owner of an ancient tavern and a lonely old miser. Collecting once on behalf of the Scouts, Oiney had opened the tavern door. Immediately a cluster of bells above the door clanged out so loudly that Oiney took to his heels in fright. On the occasion now of the Wake, he would never have dreamed of attending were it not for the fact that his granny sent him to collect a little brown jug that Doyle had promised her long years ago for some favour she had rendered him.

Oiney knocked on the front door of the tavern for quite a while until at last a window was raised in a room directly over the bar. A woman informed him that if he wished to enter he would have to do so by the arched entry and lane to the back of the house. He did so, passing a small grey van parked in the yard. Opening the rear door which led to the kitchen he went in and climbed the stairs up to the parlour where the Wake was being held.

As he might have expected Mrs Coyle and the widow Murtagh were there, glasses of sherry and porter in their hands, and sharing a wooden form with an old man, Thady McNally from the Shercock road. This veteran kept wheezing and grunting and knocking back pints of porter at a great rate. He had a claim to fame in the Guinness Book of Records for attending more funerals than any man in Ulster. A man and woman, professing to be country cousins of the deceased, sat on chairs near the head of the bed and among another small group of 'mourners' to the rear of the room Oiney recognised the bookie's clerk O'Dowd and Mrs Dignam who swept the chapel floor twice a week. After this glance at the living Oiney turned to look at the dead, and almost recoiled with the shock. Doyle was dressed in his habit all right, with his crossed pearly-white knuckles clutching a silver crucifix.

But it was the expression and particularly the position of Mr Doyle's face which so startled Oiney. The publican lay on his back but his head was turned to the wall as though he was disgusted with the present company having so much free drink at his expense. And from the little bit of his countenance that was visible, Oiney was certain that it registered the dead man's utter disapproval. Oiney could detect clearly the cold aloof scorn on Doyle's face; he wanted nothing to do, alive or dead, with this lot.

The widow Murtagh, however, was not going to allow any unkindness spoil the occasion. 'Oh my, doesn't he look grand! That month in Scotland did him the world of good. They say he collapsed with excitement at the Rangers-Celtic match in Glasgow, and never even came to to hear the final score, God bless an' save us an' keep us from harm.'

'Don't let us be morbid,' said Mrs Coyle wisely, 'for it puts a downcast spell on the best occasions an' causes indigestion. Tell you what! This honest lad Oiney with the makings of a priest in him will, if he's askèd nice, do the obligations o' carryin' new refreshments up from the bar below.'

'Me cousin, me first cousin,' added the countryman, nodding towards the corpse, 'would fully approve o' them sentiments. In moderation, of course.'

Thus the unwilling Oiney was enlisted to carry fresh drinks for the merry company. And at heart he did not like to refuse. This was one of his great failings; he had this chronic anxiety to prove himself of some use in the world. So it came to pass that although he had a great repugnance towards misers, corpses and clouds of tobacco smoke, his loyalty to Mrs Coyle, who had spoken so favourably of him, made him endure all the disagreeable elements of his many sorties, upstairs and down.

The company by this time was becoming quite maudlin. Mrs Coyle was crying. 'He was the kind man at heart, wasn't he? All that money he sent on the Foreign Missions an' the black babies an' masses for his soul. He had a conscience . . .'

'Conscience be damned,' exclaimed the widow Murtagh. 'Masses, the Missions, black babies an' what have you! Wasn't them his fire escape!'

'Fire escape?'

'Aye, fire escape. From the flames o' Hell . . .'

'Mother o' God, take care o' us!'

On one of his many sorties Oiney was startled to notice that he was being watched carefully by two men in the shadows of the Bar. He almost dropped the tray with fright.

'Oh, don't worry about us,' said the smaller of the two men, a stout jovial fellow with a magnifcent beard. 'We'll not bother you one little bit. Just carry on your business as normal as if we didn't exist. But first tell us! Who are you?'

'They call me Oiney Hoy, though I don't like it at all, an' I came up here to fetch the wee brown jug that Mr Doyle promised me granny. Mr Doyle's friends an' relations up at the Wake asked me to fetch them some drink from the Bar here . . .'

'Do you know any o' them?' asked the stranger suspiciously.

'I only know the village folk,' said Oiney, 'not the relations, not the country cousins.'

'Country cousins me eye,' exclaimed the little fellow with a laugh of great scorn. 'They're nothin' but charlatans, moochers an' chancers come here to fleece me dead father.'

Oiney's mouth opened wider with astonishment. 'Mr Doyle . . . your dead father? I didn't know Mr Doyle had a son . . .'

'Which just goes to show you that you don't know everything. Isn't that right?'

Oiney had to admit that the stranger was indeed quite right in that respect. There were some gaps in his education.

'Let me introduce ourselves,' said the jovial one smiling kindly. 'I'm Shaun Doyle, son of the lately deceased, an' this is my dear, dear friend from Shantonagh, Sheamus Tynan. All the property in this premises is mine by right, but I shall honour any agreement me father had with townsfolk like your granny. She shall have her little jug. In fact she can have all the jugs in the house . . .'

Oiney was so overcome by this wonderful gesture on the part of Mr Doyle's son that he shook the hands of both strangers warmly, though he had this peculiar feeling of having met the taller of the two men somewhere in Creevan or on the train to Lough Derg. He promised Shaun his undying friendship. Now he could clearly understand why Mr Doyle's face had been turned to the wall. The publican had correctly assessed on his deathbed in Monaghan hospital that his Wake in Creevan would be attended by parasites and chancers. Thus in anticipation of that disgusting conclusion to a worthless career, he had in one brave dying gesture turned his face away from such low company. Oiney indeed felt a great sense of Christian outrage at the indignity inflicted on a man who, whatever else his earthly failings, had donated such a proud gift as a lofty weather-cock to the chapel spire.

'I'll fetch no more drink,' he shouted in righteous anger, 'to that despicable crew.'

'On the contrary,' said Shaun, putting his arm on Oiney's shoulder, 'we shall turn the left cheek an' kill them with kindness. We'll double their allowance until their very wits fail them. Take the full tray up to them, but return here to report an' we'll surely be friends for life.'

Delighted with such a fine and glowing prospect, Oiney, carrying a loaded tray, staggered upstairs. The Wake had reached a new peak of elation with Mrs Murtagh collecting some 'souvenir' pictures from the wall of the parlour and the 'country cousins' doing their level best to restrain her. Oiney was only too glad to escape into the more wholesome atmosphere of the Bar below. Nor was he the least surprised to find that Shaun, the rightful heir of Mr Doyle, and his dear friend Sheamus had completely stripped the gantry of its contents and were piling the latter into cardboard boxes and bags which were lying in a heap by the back door. Oiney was only too delighted to assist in the collection of silver tankards, that Shaun, obviously trustful of his new friend's honesty, bestowed on him the special favour of emptying the contents of the till into a leather satchel which Sheamus graciously held out for him.

For the very first time in his young life Oiney was given a real sense of responsibility and trust, and he responded to this in a magnificent spirit of delight. His friends were more than pleased with him when he helped to carry the boxes and bags through the door and into the grey van parked in the yard. Shaun again put a friendly arm around Oiney. 'How shall I ever repay you?'

'Oh,' said Oiney warmly. 'I'm only too eager to help in a just cause. I was taught that in the Scouts.'

'And rightly so, and rightly so,' agreed Shaun. 'But Sheamus and I feel really obligated to you. We have had the deepest discussion imaginable on how we can repay our debt to you. And we have decided to offer you a grand tour of Ireland.'

Oiney stood wide-eyed in wonder. 'Do you really mean it? The Mountains of Mourne, the Hill of Tara, The Book of Kells, the Rose of Tralee and Danny Boy? Away from Creevan, the Holy Terror, and the boredom o' winter! Oh, wouldn't I just love it!' A tour of Ireland with these delightful newly found friends who trusted him as no one else did – with the exception of Jonjo perhaps. 'D'you really mean it? A tour of Ireland?'

'Of course we mean it,' said Shuan, and fearful lest Oiney change his mind, bundled him gently but quickly into the rear of the van.

Travelling in the back of a cramped little van over the bumpy by-lanes of north Monaghan in the dead of night is no promising start to the grand tour of Ireland. In the midst of his great excitement and confused thinking, Oiney found it quite difficult to keep up a conversation with Sheamus.

'What age are you, Oiney?'

'About seventeen I think. I'm not sure.'

'Not sure?'

'Me mother's dead an' me father left Ireland to dig for gold in the streets o' London. Me granny says he must have dug as far as Australia be now. He never came back.'

'D'you want to be a priest, Oiney?'

'What?' The Creevan lad wondered was he hearing right.

'I thought that perhaps you had this vocation in you.'

'Vocation? What's that?'

'The vocation. The voice o' God callin' in the wind . . . like Saint Patrick heard when he escaped from slavery in the Slemish Mountains . . . You see, Oiney. I'm a failed priest meself.'

Oiney did not know what to say. Life was full of so many surprises. 'Sure worse could've happened you.'

'Such as?'

Oiney searched wildly for an answer. 'You might,' he suggested timidly, 'you might've got ate.'

'Got what?' Sheamus turned around in the front to see if this yokel in the back was serious. Oiney's face was in deadly earnest. 'Me granny says some missionary priests were ate recently in the Amazonian rain-forests an' there was nothin' left but the stumps o' their legs. I don't like talkin' about it, God help them; if their souls were saved that's the main thing. What failed you as a priest, Sheamus?'

'It was the booze, Oiney, nothing but the booze. At first I got hooked on the altar wine, then the Benedictine, and after that anything God sent us. It nearly broke my mother's heart but I gave it up at the hinder-end. It was too late, though.'

Suddenly a great doubt flooded Oiney's mind. Here he was with two strangers travelling through the wilds of Ireland in the middle of the night, a van full of whiskey and beer, and him talking to a failed priest as well, on the eve of a grand tour of Ireland. It was more like a strange dream and too, too much to believe. 'Shaun?'

'What is it, Oiney?'

'I want you to tell me the truth, Shaun? How could you be Doyle's son when I never even saw you once in the village, and nobody ever mentioned to me that Doyle had a son? Answer me that before we go any further!'

'Honest to God,' said Shaun, 'but aren't you the oul' doubtin' Thomas? In all fairness however, you ask a very observant, pertinent question an' one that shall have an answer, no beatin' about the bush, no dodgin' it, an' no quibblin'. I think, Sheamus, we should enlighten Oiney a little more. We really hadn't much time back at the tavern, but, you see, here we are.'

Oiney immediately agreed on that point. There was no disputing it. 'Here we are.'

'Are you listenin', Oiney?'

'I'm listenin', Shaun, with both ears.'

'Good. You see it's like this. Me mother worked as a skivvy for Doyle for years in Creevan before you were born, Oiney. She slaved away, a poorly paid servant. A more pious prig of a degenerate Irishman the green fields of Erin never held than the same Doyle! Me mother was a good-lookin' girsha in them days when the dirty bowser took advantage of her in the bottlin' shed in the back-yard yonder . . .'

'He did not,' exclaimed the awestruck Oiney, unwilling to believe that such filthy things happened in holy Catholic Ireland, especially from a man who had donated a weather-cock to the chapel.

'Oh, I know it's a terrible shock to an innocent chiseleur like yerself, Oiney,' said Shaun, 'but God's me judge. An' Sheamus there that was in Holy Orders himself will vouch for it.'

'Me hand up to God, but it's the gospel-truth,' agreed Sheamus, even though the low roof of the van prevented his hand from stretching very high.

'Tell him, Shaun, about Doyle's takin' your poor mother to Dublin! Tell him that!'

'I was coming to that Oiney. When me mother was expectin' her baby, the oul' wretch smuggled her out o' Creevan to a maternity home run by the nuns in the suburbs o' Dublin, where I was born. He gave the nuns a brave few quid to look after us for a time, but on no account were we ever to set foot in Creevan again. He put on the oul' Adam act an' left me poor mother to provide for herself an' me. I grew up in the Liberties o' Dublin, an' even when I was a lot younger than yerself Oiney, I was bundlin' firewood an' sellin' scrap in the back-streets. I grew up a harum-scarum vagabond. Me mother, God bless her in them days, became a staunch rebel, Oiney. But though she hated the memory o' Cromwell, the memory o' Doyle was even worse to her. I vowed one day I'd get evens with the villain. When I began to grow up, I often stole quietly back into Creevan to take stock o' the situation. An' when Doyle began to ail, I got me dear friend from Shantonagh to wire me on the situation . . .'

'That's where I came in,' said Sheamus proudly. 'I gave Shaun the nod when the oul' fellow was on his deathbed in Monaghan. An' you know who I had that information from? D'you recall meetin' a stranger, Oiney, on the Cootehill road when you were out pickin' shamrocks?'

'What an amazin' world surely,' exclaimed Oiney. 'I knew I had seen you before. I simply cannot believe it. Wasn't I right?'

'You were surely,' agreed Sheamus, 'but then Shaun an' I realised your amazin' intelligence early on. The very minute we set eyes on you. That's a lad, if given a chance, could turn the destiny of Ireland and change the textbooks of history. Isn't that a fact, Shaun?'

'Without a shadow o' doubt,' said Shaun, 'you have the potential. But not to lose the thread o' me story. I went to me dyin' father's bedside in Monaghan hospital and asked him to bestow me nathural rights, but divil the budge from the stubborn oul' bugger, though the gates o' Hell were starin' him in the face. He'd rather leave his worldly gear to the chapel an' masses for the repose of his worthless soul. That's the kind of dirty oul' reprobate we've been raisin' in Ireland since they murdhered James Connolly an' the like. Doyle gave me one long mean look and turned to the wall. After that rigor mortis set in.'

'Holy Mary, mother o' God,' cried Oiney, 'but you're right. Every word of it. That's the real reason why his face

34

was to the wall. It wasn't Mrs Coyle an' the widow Murtagh he was rebuffin'. It was you. It was you, Shaun.'

'God knows, Oiney,' said Shaun, 'you're the bright wee fella right enough. No wonder Sheamus thinks you've the makings of a priest in you. What a loss to the church an' the bench in a scholar like you. So I came to Creevan as you know know to get me share before the Bishop of Clogher grabs the lot.'

Oiney sat in the back of the van, his mind completely dazed by these strange and terrible revelations. This was not the sweet little island, dear little island he had sung about at the school on the hill in Creevan.

At the Border

It was almost midnight when the van drew to a halt under a dark archway of beech trees. The three occupants were glad to descend, Oiney especially, from his cramped condition. He stood gazing at the wonderful pattern of stars visible in the heavens through some of the upper branches. His more mundane companions on the other hand stared anxiously at the lit window of a little hut perched on the side of the road about two hundred yards ahead. Oiney could not hear them clearly. Then Shaun approached him. 'Oiney?'

'Yes, Shaun?'

'What a lovely euphonious name!'

'You what,' said the Creevan lad, for his vocabulary was meagre.

'Euphonious, sweet soundin', melodious! Like the bells o' Shandon they sound so grand on the pleasant waters o' the river Lee. That's melodious an' so is Oiney. Could even be Chinese – Oi Nee Hoi! A cut above your Pat an' Mick or even Larry. Oiney Hoy! How originally refreshing! How did you ever acquire it?'

Then and there Oiney unburdened his soul, the immense granary of his youthful experiences. Under a moonlit sky and a great white cloud that came tumbling over the plain of Muirtheme and the shadowy peak of Slieve Gullion, he told Shaun the tale of the Holy Terror and the recent visit to Lough Derg and how Ireland would sink in the Atlantic five years before the end of the world.

'What an amazin' tale, Oiney, and it only goes to prove that wonders never cease in Ireland. I'm learnin' things this night I never knew existed. And that fearful bit about Ireland sinkin'. That should be brought to the attention

36

of the Minister of Fisheries who attends to floods an' the like, and maybe to Town and Country Plannin', for they like to be informed as well. An' my God, that oul' granny o' yours, she needs a department all to herself. She doesn't deserve a lad of such knowledge as you, or even the wee brown jug you were takin' her. Wasn't it the blessin' o' God in the heavens up there that crossed our paths!'

'Friends,' exclaimed Oiney in a voice of gratitude to match the immensity of the occasion. 'How can I ever thank you enough for enterin' me life at such a vital moment when I was being sucked into the whirlpool of an inane village life – funerals, pilgrimages, wakes, prayers, publicans an' what have you? I realise now I'm only beginnin' to live. Shaun, just tell me! Tell me! What is life?' He imagined this so profound that he thought it worthwhile repeating. 'Just what is life?'

'Now you're askin',' said Shaun, who had given some thought to the subject in Crumlin Jail, and had even consulted a Jesuit at University College Dublin, without any deep satisfaction. He steered Oiney away from that debateable marshland. 'A chap I knew said that Life was the opposite of Death but not quite! But Oiney, never mind small details, we're still friends, aren't we?'

'How, how,' said Oiney with great fervour, 'can I ever repay you?'

Shaun put that warm comradely arm around Oiney once more. 'We wouldn't dream of acceptin' any payment, Oiney, but you might help us with one of those little corporeal works o' mercy which our Church is always exhortin' us to perform for the good of our souls . . .'

'And the souls in Purgatory,' Oiney piously reminded him.

'Them too,' said Shaun, drawing Oiney aside and pointing to the little wooden hut in the distance. 'A very, very good friend of ours lives in that hut, that small abode. Unfortunately the poor fella's mind is slightly deranged. He's the sad victim of amazin' fantasies an' casts himself in a variety of roles like a stage actor. Sometimes he is a bishop, or a deep-sea captain, or the conductor of an orchestra, an' he won't brook contradiction. He even dresses up for the part. Presently he believes he's a Customs Officer . . .'

'How ridiculous can you get,' said Oiney shaking his head. 'An important man like a Customs Officer in a silly little hut not fit even for a tinker. But poor fellow, it's not his fault.'

'You're right Oiney, as usual, an' I honestly blame the moon for most of our friend's troubles. If there were no full moons he'd be quite normal. Mind you, he's eccentric, an' can be a surly customer if his silly sense o' loyalty an' duty is challenged. Like Nelson an' Napoleon he carries the daft personal onus of an Empire that'll prosper or perish with or without any o' them. Our poor friend now has the strange obsession that it is his God-given duty to supervise what he foolishly imagines to be the Irish Border.'

Oiney could not resist a titter of laughter at the poor fool's expense. 'Imagine him holding such a silly, silly notion! Still, there's no accountin' for extravagant ideas, is there? There was this peasant girl in Carrick who stuck a pitch-fork in a dung-hill an' cried out that she was Joan of Arc. They took her to Monaghan asylum because she didn't know one word o' French. An' there was this other man who . . .'

'Quite so,' said Shaun impatiently, 'it's a cruel world but let's stick to one subject at a time, shall we? Sheamus an' I would like to present our dear friend in the hut with a little token of our great esteem. A bottle o' the best brand o' whiskey, an' this other little parcel, a clock. Convey our warmest regards but undher no circumstances let him leave the hut to thank us! We'll drive quietly up the road an' you can join us later at the bridge yonder. Will you do that for us?'

'Certainly I will,' said the eager Oiney, 'for I never in me mortal life met two men with such innate goodness in them. First you give them unworthy moochers in the pub all the dhrink in the world. Then you offer me a grand tour of Ireland. An' now you send gifts to an unfortunate creature who values life so low that he imagines he is a Customs Officer. I'll tell you this much. You two are kindness personified.'

'Treat the poor fellow with great care, Oiney,' warned Shaun, 'an' for God's sake don't let him out on the road!'

'Just leave it in my capable hands,' said the confident Oiney.

A few second later the Creevan lad, on his mission of mercy, emerged from the archway of trees. He was whistling a merry tune that Jonjo had taught him when a tall, sour-faced individual answered his knock on the door. 'What hour o' the night d'you take this to be,' he growled. Oiney saw the strange fellow glare at him wickedly. As Shaun had predicted, the daft hermit of the hut was dressed in the rather plain uniform of a Customs Officer. He also wore a little Hitlerite moustache, which was a handsome match for his nasty temper.

'I haven't got a watch, mister,' answered Oiney, 'but be the look o' the stars it's on the far side o' midnight.'

'You're a smart little puppy,' snarled the Customs.

'Indeed, I'm not,' said Oiney modestly, 'for me marks at school were only middlin'.'

'Listen, clever lad! I've met your kind before an' I want no palaver with you, d'you hear! What have you to declare?'

'What have I to declare? What have I to declare?' cried Oiney, thoroughly aroused by this time. 'I declare to God you're the carnaptious oul' eejit, an' a sight worse than the Ticket Inspector on the train to Lough Derg. Surely I only brought this bottle o' whiskey an' a present . . .'

'So you're smugglin' illicit whiskey, are you?'

'It's a present for you.'

'Ah, so it's bribery as well. Smugglin' whiskey an' bribery! I wouldn't like to be in your shoes, me bucko. This is the Customs, you know.'

'This is the Customs! This is the Customs!' Oiney could not resist mimicking him. 'Well, if them are your Customs I don't like them one wee bit, for your Customs are terrible an' your grammar atrocious.'

'Listen, you fool,' shouted the angry official, 'you are at the Border, the Border I tell you. Don't you know it?'

'I'm at the border all right,' said Oiney, 'the border-line of me patience.'

At that very moment the van passed the hut at great speed and the Customs Officer made a tremendous effort to rush out onto the road to sight the smugglers or at least get a glimpse of their number-plates. But Oiney hemmed him in gabbing away unmercifully at a great rate, reciting nursery rhymes and even jabberwocky to confuse and paralyse the poor man. Anything to prevent him from going out onto the road.

'You'll pay for this,' roared the irate official, several large veins protruding on his neck and forehead. 'You'll pay for this. Smuggling, bribery and now obstruction in the course o' duty.'

It was clear to Oiney now that the daft hermit was indeed obsessed with his strange notions. 'But I'm forced to conclude,' said the Creevan lad, 'that Shaun an' Sheamus are somewhat mistaken in your worth. You're not the nice harmless fella they think you are. You haven't just got a little weakness o' mind. You're an ill-tempered baiste of a man, an' I'm just takin' the whiskey an' clock presents back to Shaun . . .'

'Did you say "clock"?' shouted the Customs, turning pale.

'Aye, the whiskey an' the clock.'

Oiney now saw the Customs man go really berserk, throwing his peak-cap and overcoat over the clock. Then he grabbed Oiney by the neck and arm and dragged him into a deep ditch on the far side of the road.

'Begod, I'm holdin' on to you at least, me bucko.' Just then there was a terrific explosion and the little hut took off. The great white tumbling cloud from Slieve Gullion had drifted over by Fermanagh and Sligo, and there in the clear moonlight, Oiney saw the hut twirl and twirl in the sky until it landed in a field beside some bog-land.

'Holy mother o' God, mister,' cried the astonished Oiney in a hushed voice. 'Did you see that? Did you see that?'

'Don't come the innocent buffoon with me,' snapped the surly official. 'Don't tell me you knew nothin' about it! Don't pretend you didn't know this was the Irish border!'

'Honest to God, mister,' said poor Oiney in a voice of pathos. 'Honest to God, mister, how could I know? Sure the leafy trees are the same, beech an' lime an' oak on both sides, an' the birds the same hoppin' from tree to bush, an' the flowin' river the same north an' south an' the green grass the same on both sides. Ah, bad luck on them pair o' villains, Shaun an' Sheamus, for deceivin' me . . .'

The Customs Officer gave a great guffaw of sheer disbelief. 'Don't tell me that you expected the grass to turn orange or blue in the Six Counties! Tell that to the Judge an' see what he says! Smuggling, Bribery, Obstruction and now Terrorism. At least we've got you me bucko, an' we'll make you squawk. By the time you come out o' Crumlin or Armagh you'll be older than Rip Van Winkle's grandfather. You will that.'

Oiney in Jail

If Oiney had found it difficult to pass his time during the winter seasons in Creevan, that was surely a life of gusto and daring in contrast to the bleak walls and even bleaker faces of the warders of Armagh jail, the prison in which he now so abjectly found himself. Coming as he did from the south of Ireland, although still within the great ancient province of Ulster, all the prison staff hated and despised him. A nasty warder nicknámed 'Shankill' particularly so. To that fine specimen of northern justice, a southern Irishman was a symbol of everything obnoxious in life – the Pope, rosary beads, the Blessed Virgin, the Celtic football team, Lourdes, the holy water, De Valera and the rocky road to Dublin. 'Shankill' knew only two songs, 'The Sash' and 'The Ould Orange Flute', one flag, The Union Jack with its Red Hand crest, and one way to deal with Catholics, – down them!

He now opened the peephole in the door of Oiney's cell to have another close look at the strange creature recently hauled in from the bleak boglands of Eire. What on earth was the crazy fellow up to? He saw the frantic Oiney, a pencil stub in hand, running around the small cell from corner to corner and at the same time making peculiar gestures. What annoyed 'Shankill' in particular was that these gestures seemed to have some connection with Papish rituals and greatly resembled the sign of the Cross. The eager glow on Oiney's young face vexed the warder so much that, seizing his riot stick, he rushed into the cell.

'What the bloody hell are you up to?'

'It's just a pencil,' said the startled Oiney.

'Pencil me eye! No man rushes around the cell with a pencil stub making weird signs. Don't take me for an eejit!'

'It's a game I'm playin'.'

'Game you're playing? What game?'

'I call it "guess where",' explained Oiney.

'Guess where? Don't talk bloody riddles to me!'

'If you calm down, mister, I'll explain. Life gets a little boring if you're in this lone cell hour after hour so I made up this little game of "guess where" to pass the time. It's really simple. D'you see that little fly that's now sittin' on the chamber pot. Well, in a second or two he'll be up an' flyin' about, so I try to guess where he's goin' to land on the wall and I mark the spot with a wee cross. It's excitin' isn't it? Wouldn't you like a shot? Have a go, mister! I know you'd like it.'

Absentmindedly, 'Shankill' accepted the pencil stub and then suddenly realising his mistake threw it on the floor and stamped on it with his studded heel.

'Would I like a shot? Would I like a shot, you priest-ridden half-wit,' he snarled. 'Guess where! Guess where I'll put this stick in a minit, you village moron. Clean up your cell this instant for the head-shrinker's comin' to see you and Christ knows he has a case on his hands! You need him surely.' The warder then, to make it easier for Oiney to tidy up, tipped the contents of the chamber pot over the floor with his heel before slamming the cell door.

It was little kind gestures like this which endeared 'Shankill' to all the prisoners. He also had a very worthy record of previous socially useful employment. Prior to his present edifying position he had been a debt collector for a rich finance company in north Belfast and before that he had been for several months a zealous and well-paid scab labourer in the shipyards. These prestigious posts had provided excellent references for his advancement to the Prison Service, but not nearly so influential in doing so as the fact that every Twelfth of July his hands were swollen and bloody from battering the big Lambeg drum to summon the Loyalist tribes to the Orange fields at Finaghy.

Shortly after his footsteps had faded in the corridor, a lean, chinless face stared at Oiney through the spyhole. Tucker Wayne, the prison psychiatrist, was a very tall thin eccentric man dressed in a white, frowsy half-length cotton coat with dark-rimmed, thick-set glasses. He had the wary habit of making copious notes at the spyhole before actual contact with the prisoner. 'Shankill' returned to open the cell for him. One of Wayne's peculiar traits was moments of extreme truth followed by sheer gibberish.

'So you are Hoy. Don't stand up! Mind if I sit?' He planked himself on the low bed without awaiting an answer. His long legs made an angular bridge at the knees with the wall opposite. 'Not really much room here, is there? Now tell me what I can do for you: I'm your psychiatrist.'

'What would that be?' asked the puzzled Oiney, for this was the first time in his life to hear the word.

'Well now, I'll explain it as simple as I can. Let me see. I pry into the human brain box . . .'

'Not mine you don't,' exclaimed the alarmed Oiney, leaping to the top of the bed. 'This is one brain box you aren't goin' to pry into an' that's for sure!'

Mr Wayne made a sharp entry in his notebook: Unsocial . . . chronic anxiety neurosis verging on paranoia . . . extremely suspicious . . . ears twitching and fingers fidgety. 'Tell me, young man, what made you blow up the hut? You can be honest with me. D'you hate Orangemen?'

'I hardly know what an Orangeman is and I doubt if he knows himself. I was taught at Creevan school that all human beings were created in the image o' God and I believe that except mebbe for that ugly brute staring in the side of the door there . . .'

'Let me at him,' shouted the angry intruder who was none other than our friend 'Shankill', doing his usual eavesdropping. 'Let me at him till I knock his melt in!'

'Shut that door immediately or I'll report the matter,' the psychiatrist ordered before turning to Oiney. 'So you see, laddie, I'm really your friend. Confess everything to your dear friend and I'll see if I can have you certified.'

'Certified? What's that?'

'It's just a little valuable note written by me and signed by two other doctors which makes you hold no responsibility for the terrible crimes you committed. It will make you feel almost innocent.'

'But I am innocent,' Oiney protested. 'Honest to God up there, I did nothin'. I was only delivering a message. I can't recall a single wrong thing I did since I was enticed out of Creevan. Honest. I swear it on my granny's life I was only doin' a message.'

Despite Oiney's offer of such a high stake as his granny's valuable life, Mr Wayne looked singularly unconvinced and made another entry in his notebook: Prisoner admits lapsing into comatose condition . . . but pretends no cognition of wrong-doing . . . subconscious guilt transference to a dependent relative – his unfortunate grandmother . . .

Then the psychiatrist stared into Oiney's bewildered blue eyes for a full minute until the poor prisoner thought he recognised what was afoot. At the old school on the hill in Creevan, when two boys quarrelled over which of them was telling the truth, they stared long and hard into each other's eyes, the first one to blink being the liar. Mr Wayne gazed in amazement at the unblinking Oiney and then averted his eyes towards his notebook.

'Caught you out,' shouted Oiney in triumph. 'Now who's tellin' the truth?'

Strange fellow, wrote the psychiatrist, reflex reactions completely abnormal . . . optically non-existent . . .

'So you see,' added Oiney still in a grand mood of triumph, 'I'm absolutely innocent.'

'Rest assured, lad. The Court won't hold your innocence against you. It might even help in getting your sentence reduced to ten or fifteen years and take into consideration the fact that it was not your fault you were born a Catholic and an Irishman with all the criminal propensities in the blood.'

Since the very inquisitive Mr Wayne, apart from having nothing better to do with his time, had formally to justify a little the fat salary he was receiving, he visited Oiney's cell quite frequently with his black notebook. On the second occasion he took Oiney's pulse and blood pressure and then made the Creevan lad lie stretched on the bed while he swung a copper ball on a piece of string above his victim's eyes. He then spoke in such a slow, sonorous drone that he almost fell asleep himself: 'Take it easy ...Relax ... Lie back and relax ... That's better ... I want you to go back in time ... Go back slowly in time ... Slowly ... slowly ... as far as your memory can ... Tell me everything!'

'Blurp,' said Oiney. 'Me granny told me I had the wind often and me back was blue from her thumpin' me.'

'Carry on ... Carry on ... you're doin' fine ... Continue from there!'

'Eeny ... meanie ... miny mo,' said Oiney, '... and this wee piggie cried wee, wee, wee all the way home!'

'Superb! Superb,' exclaimed Mr Wayne gleefully, certain he was on the brink of wonderful confessions.

'I'm sorry,' said Oiney, sitting up. 'I can't remember a thing. I think that's because I was born very young, too young altogether, so much so that I can't remember a thing more until I was three years old and standin' cryin' me eyes out with this big banana in me hand.'

'Crying? Is that because you were spoiled?'

'No, it just looked so nice and yellow like a big sweetie, but no one took the skin off. Those first three years of me life are a blank to me, an' after that me granny an' the master kept cloutin' me so much that any sense I may have had was knocked out o' me. So I'm not much of a guinea-pig, am I?'

Tucker Wayne was not to be put off so easily. 'Ah, this granny of yours. Tell me more about her! I'll tell you what. I'll leave a notebook and pen for you and you just jot down your early memories of her and Creevan. Will you do that and I'll see if I can help you?'

'Well, I'm sure I could do worse an' won't it help to pass the time if you keep that other quare fella out o' me cell!'

'I'll have a sharp word with him,' promised the psychiatrist before leaving.

In the weeks that followed Oiney began to fill in his notebook, first with doodle caricatures of Shaun and Sheamus, the Customs Man, Tucker Wayne and 'Shankill';

then he began his own story as best as the poor fellow could . . .

I was born in Creevan at the back o' beyont in the heart of Ireland. As true as God's me judge I did no man or woman any wrong except maybe that holy water in the lemonade bottle but it cured them anyway and God pitying me good intentions who knows changed it to the rale thing I was brought up a Catholic because no one said I was any different and I don't suppose they asked me. Me granny was never done callin' me a beggar's get and oiney hoy that I don't remember me own name for the clouts I got from her and the masters though the lady teacher was good as gold and used to give the poorest barefoot boys a sup out of her own milk an I was told I had this invisible soul and the guardian angel perched on top of me right hand shoulder all the time though God knows I never felt the weight of a feather and it must've been dumb or in a terrible huff for it never as much as bid me the time of day I mind tempting it and God a bit to prove they were there but the only answer I got was the empty wind sighing in the birch trees and the great walnut tree down by the edge of Dromore river they said God made the lovely flowers and the birds and the bees but he also made the rats and the fleas to bite and wasps to sting and lightening to kill and often I felt he was as far away in Heaven as me own father wherever he is on earth I saw a lot of poor people in Creevan and everyone so much on their knees that sometimes you'd believe that there was no job worth having on earth and they all wanted to go up above with their Amens, Amens I often got the blame for things I never done just like this customs hut I got this terrible picture of Hell and I'm shocking afraid of roasting there if you don't die with a true confession on your soul and only then with a love of God you've never seen its an awful worry and a great puzzling thing on the big globe of the world called earth that they say spins through space at a mile a minute. Me granny the Holy Terror is as big a mystery to me as God almost but I never saw her do the things that me cousin Sheamus swore she did that night in the van the years maybe changed her but she did buy me the green gansey and took me to Blackrock to jump up

*and down in the sea and to Lough Derg with her corns
and bunions and lemonade bottle when the daft ticket man
had a look at me turned-up trousers the shame it brought
to me red face them terrible curses too she said on Sunday
at the door with God and Robert Emmet on the mantelpiece
looking down on her and hearing every word she said the
Almighty forgive her one day and rest her poor soul isn't
she all I have with her full needle of insulin piercing her
riddled arm every single day in life for the diabetes and
never a rest for her mind of torment and that rogue Jemmy
M'Gurk often taking a lend of her I'm sure you could save
your invisible soul in Creevan as much as in the Lakes of
Killarney or Galway bay where Shaun and Sheamus swore
blind they were taking me Me granny told me that Ireland
is going to sink in the wild Atlantic five years before the end
of the world and that ghosts run mad about the church and
chapel graveyards on All Souls Night and noone should cut
the lone fairy tree in Lennon's meadow for the wee folk will
climb into your bed at night and jag your bare feet with the
cut branches and she said that every night at the stroke of
midnight the black headless horses and coach of the great
Leslie family dash through the dark streets of Creevan to
the family vault at the back of the Castle but I don't hear
or see them with me head well under the blankets and there's
a secret tunnel under the hollow sound on the brae at the
haunted woods of Knockmaddy and Terry of the Hills can't
cross a chapel door because one of his ancestors informed on
a Mass Rock priest in the penal days and got five pounds
for him being put to death and that Captain Prunty now
walks with a jerky limp of his right leg he got from God
for turning over the dead corpses of his poor enemies with
his foot oh, you'd never guess half the great things she told
me in that old kitchen of ours among the birch trees . . .*

It was a few weeks later that Mr Wayne collected the
completed manuscript with all its blots, squiggles and torn
leaves. The psychiatrist seemed in such a depressed mood
that he could scarcely speak. He was so downcast that

Oiney, forgetting his own plight, tried to console the unfortunate gentleman: 'Look on the bright side, Mr Wayne! You haven't died a winter yet, have you? Every cloud has a silver lining an' far-off hills are green. Never put off till tomorrow what you can do today an' too many cooks spoil the broth, don't they?'

The disconsolate psychiatrist shook his head. 'Penelope is no cook. She can't even grate cheese. She's the worst cook in Christendom. But it isn't just that. It's her blustering conceit. She took this damned trumpet to Portadown on the Orange Walk and insisted on going ahead of the Bands. She nearly drowned out the big drums and made a right clown of me when I tried to intervene. She hates my literary tastes as well, my favourite writers, Zane Gray, Mickey Spillane. Wants me to read the Bible more and devote myself to writing some anti-Catholic pamphlets. She makes me feel, how shall I put it, a little inadequate. The longer I live with her the more I feel like the quack I am. What do I know about the science of medicine? The Infirmary I run here is just a sham, a halfway transit camp, nothing less, between the jail, the morgue or the asylum. If ever the notice "Abardon Hope All Ye Who Enter" should be written anywhere it is here. I'm nothing but a charlatan, lad, a quack!'

Oiney, of course, had long suspected this but his truly gentle nature made him abhor self-denigration in others. Besides, a jail is depressing enough without its inmates and staff becoming unduly morose and adding to the gloom. 'Don't lower your self-esteem, Mr Wayne! I'm sure God has some purpose for you somewhere. You might apply for the Foreign Missions. Africa and parts of Asia they say are so short of medical people that they might even take you . . . It's only a suggestion . . .'

'I'll tell you what I'll do. I'll go straight home and put that bloody trumpet in the river or the fire. That's what I'll do.'

'Shankill' stood at the open cell door with a mean snigger on his smug countenance. After Wayne had gone down the corridor in a rage, Oiney heard the warder croak, 'Burn it or drown it, like the brave Orange Flute in Dungannon, it will still play "Protestant Boys".'

On a visit a week later Tucker Wayne was in an even worse state. He almost collapsed on Oiney's bed. 'There's been a calamity,' he groaned. 'I'm just the purveyor of disasters. That's what I am.'

'Has Penelope left you?' asked Oiney sympathetically.

'No such luck,' growled the visitor. 'This latest calamity occurred last Friday in Newry, a fatal day for me. My secretary and I were having a quiet confab in a private hotel, you know the sort of thing, urgent business and all that, when it dawned on me that I had left the car door open with my briefcase inside.'

'And it was stolen?'

'The worst of it was that your notebook was in that case! My God, you'll be shocked when you hear the complete story. You'll be frantic!'

'Oh, don't worry about that, mister,' said the calm Oiney. 'Them notes o' mine are better lost. Them childish ravings are best forgotten. I just wrote down the first thing came into me head.'

'Oh, it's much, much worse than that, lad. It's a calamity of the first degree. Them Nationalist folk of Newry and the town's brimming with them have laid their foul hands on the notebook and they've published every line you wrote in the local paper with a brief but damning preface of their own. There: you may as well go ahead and read it! Here!'

He handed Oiney the paper and the Creevan lad sat down on the edge of the bed to read it aloud; slowly his expression changed from wonder to downright consternation and anger at the contents of the preface to his own story:

JAILED INNOCENCE

The RUC and six county junta must surely be scraping the bottom of the barrel when they are holding in Armagh Gaol without charge or trial a poor harmless nonentity called Oiney Hoy, a lad from the obscure village of Creevan in the County Monaghan. We have in our possession (we will not reveal from what source it arrived with us) a personal document written by this poor clodhopper;

he describes in it scores of rather pathetic incidents in his bizarre existence. We are not saying that the young man is certifiable, though the authorities may use this course, but any honest, intelligent person after reading the unique document objectively can only be alarmed at the state of the young man's mind. We merely request our readers to judge for themselves as they read on, giving the unfortunate fellow the benefit of their Christian charity, not forgetting that surely he is one of God's own.

THE EDITOR.

With great indignation and disgust Oiney threw the newspaper onto the cell floor. 'How dare they call me names like "one of God's own",' he stormed. 'I resemble that remark!'

'Resent, you mean,' said Mr Wayne helpfully.

'Whatever you like to call it,' said Oiney in a huff. 'And I'll tell them this much. I'm not a poor clodhopper and I never was. I never hopped a clod in me life. Never! Definitely not. An' what do they mane be "nonentity"? Usin' big words to baffle me. That's them! I don't like their insinuations, not one wee bit. One o' God's own indeed! Sure, we're all one o' God's own!'

The Holy Terror's Revenge

Meanwhile, back in Creevan, the sad demented granny was raging. Not only had the daft gasson not returned with her little brown jug, he had failed to return at all. And, since he had been in Doyle's public house the night it was cleaned out, he would certainly have some explaining to do. The Holy Terror was so angry with him that she called him all the wicked names that she knew in English, and when these ran out she summoned up all the abusive epithets that had lingered over from her youth in the Carrick hills. Even the memory of the original Oiney from those parts returned to her in a much more favourable light than the terrible amadhaun she had raised. She could not even pass up the chapel brae either without that inquisitive sexton Jonjo asking her about his lost pal's whereabouts.

She softened a good deal, however, when the terrible news reached her that Oiney was in the hands of the Royal Ulster Constabulary and Armagh Jail; all her fury then was directed towards what she fiercely described as 'them black-coated haythens with grim visage'. Quite often in her wrath she had a glance at the large picture of Robert Emmet in the Dock and she now felt more certain than ever that like that great hero of Ireland, Oiney would almost certainly end up on the gallows tree. So she stormed up and down the braes of Creevan, determined as she was at all costs to prevent Oiney going into the history books and patriotic ballads of Ireland.

Living quite near to her home in Creevan was a crafty cobbler, Jemmy McGurk. Jemmy, for reasons of his poverty and accursed drouth, had occasionally taken harmless advantage of the old woman's paranoia. He excused himself on the grounds that he was allaying her daft anxiety, but at the same time he never refused the grateful coin she often gave him for his services. One day, for example, he had answered her loud impatient knocking on his door.

'Jemmy, Jemmy McGurk, have you such a thing as a good spade or a sharp-edged shovel in your possession?'

'The best in Ireland, Mam.'

'Well, you know that villain Mooney, that lives next to me?'

'Is it Mooney the squint-eyed spalpeen you mane?'

'None other. Well, he's tryin' to get at me undher the wall that joins our houses . . .'

'The bloody blackguard! Shure, nothin's sacred to him.'

'Tell you, Jemmy, I'll give you a pound note if you take your spade and dig down undher me coal-hole an' meet him halfway in his. Will you do that for me, Jemmy?'

'I will surely, Mam, an' what's more I'll knock the livin' daylights out o' his corrugated head an' his lantern jaws.'

'Good man, Jemmy, an' the pound apart I'll light a holy candle for you in the chapel.'

'Never mind the pound or the candle. Mooney's kind is the ruin of Ireland an' the plague o' civilisation. I'll settle the randy oul' rascal. Never mind the pound, Mam, or the candle. A glass o' whiskey will suffice for the day. Don't worry, I'll sort him.'

So Jemmy took his spade over his shoulder like a peat-bog mountaineer and disappeared into the depths of the dark coal-hole. He stayed there for about five minutes battering his spade against the hard stone wall and yelling out as if he was in mortal conflict with Old Nick himself. Then wiping a little coal dust on his brow he emerged wearing a cute grin of triumph: 'That cooked his goose, Mam. That put the fear o' God in Mooney for good. If you hear as much as a squeak from him from now on, he's a goner. Tell him that from yours truly!'

Now it happened in the month following Oiney's arrest at the border, the Holy Terror found a big round torch battery near her doorstep, and never having seen the likes before was certain that Mooney was up to his tricks again, this time to blow her up. She was frantic when she called on Jemmy with the suspect cylinder held at arm's length. 'Jemmy, Jemmy, what in God's name is this dangerous contraption doin' on me doorstep? Is he tryin' to murdher me? Has he no respect for life or limb?'

'Ah, bejasus Mam,' said Jemmy, 'that Mooney fella is goin' to exthremes surely. But let me handle this, Mam.' He took the battery from her hand and held it gingerly. 'Have you a spare can o' wather, cold wather an' we'll soon make it defunct. That'll defeat Mooney's intent if he's thinkin' you're so aisy disposed of.' The Holy Terror gave a great sigh of relief when she saw the wicked object submerged.

'Three days an' three nights in that can and an odd Hail Mary over it will take the sting out of its tail,' Jemmy assured her. 'An' then if you like you can throw it on the dung-heap.'

That night the old woman kept brooding. Her thoughts then suddenly switched from the spalpeen Mooney next door to an even greater enemy, the Governor of Armagh Jail who was holding her gormless grandson, Oiney, in wrongful custody. After all, the latter was only a daft gasson, just a couple of years out of short trousers and still wet behind the ears. That mouth of his always open, catching flies. My God, she thought, if only I could lay hands on the amadhaun I'd knock sense into that great gap between his ears, mother o' God forgive me, him just a clumsy slip of a lad, never seen his father and his poor ma, me daughter, rushin' off to join the harp playin' holy angels. Imagine that brute of a Governor holdin' her innocent gasson. In her fury a fiendish thought struck her.

Next morning she arose early and hastened to Jemmy McGurk's door. 'It's an aisy five pounds for you, Jemmy.'

'What's that Mam?' asked the puzzled Jemmy, who never failed to be amused by her strange requests.

'You said three days and three nights in the can, didn't you?'

'I did indeed.'

'So it's still alive.'

'It is,' said Jemmy, wondering what was coming next.

'Well, Jemmy, there's a whole five pounds for you if you take that bomb out, dry it well, an' we'll post it in a package to them dirty Orange crew who are holdin' poor Oiney ransom. Do that, Jemmy, an' there's a good five pound note in your pocket!'

Jemmy hesitated a minute or two to consider the risk. Then he decided that it was a fairly harmless adventure, and at the very worst a hoax. He agreed to take a chance, not for five pounds but that the two of them would have a drink together in Ward's pub. He dried the battery and wrapped it well in a brown package. It was the Holy Terror herself who wrote the enclosed note in her own best squiggly capitals:

TO THE GOVERNOR OF ARMAGH JAIL, SIX COUNTIES, NORTHERN IRELAND. I'M GIVING YOU TWENTY FOUR HOURS YOU ORANGE VARMINT TO LET THE DACINT BOY, OINEY, OUT OF YOUR VILE CLUTCHES. IF YOU DON'T I WILL SEND A BIGGER BOMB TO BLOW YOUS ALL TO HELL TO JOIN YOUR RELATIONS.
SIGNED 'FAITH OF OUR FATHERS'

Then she got Jonjo to address and post the parcel, telling him it was a gift for the Governor to pass on to Oiney. After a drink with Jemmy McGurk, she returned home to wait the great news that a hole had been blown in Armagh Jail wall out of which poor Oiney could climb and return home to Creevan where she would kill him herself.

A few days later, instead of good news she had a visit from the Civic Guard Sergeant Pat Oats and Spoonbait his colleague, who came to arrest her and Jemmy. There was a great commotion in the street.

'Bad cess to you, Pat Oats,' she shouted, 'take your dirty big paws off a dacint woman that kept God's commandments a sight betther nor anyone else in Creevan. An' take that sourpuss sniveller Spoonbait back with you to the barracks or betther still to Lynch's pub where yous two are always loiterin' with intent!'

'This is a very serious matther, Mam,' said Pat Oats grandly.

'Serious me arse,' she retorted. 'If yous were doin' your duty an' caught the ones inveiglin' Oiney, yous might be worth half your pay. Instead you've nothin' betther to do with your time than hound and harass a respectable an' God-fearin' woman o' Creevan!'

'Come along with Jemmy,' Spoonbait tried to cajole her. 'Come an' we'll sort it out quietly at the Barracks!'

'Sort out the shite at the tail of your shirt, Mr Spoonbait,' she cried, 'with that hawk-nose o' yours dippin' your snot into everyone's business. If either o' yous had the guts of a sparrow yous'd be up there in the Black North causin' repercussions an' not leavin' a poor woman to sort the buggers out. I'll tell yous somethin' me buckoes. Yous'll shift Creevan Market House afore yous budge me, or that I'll be seen walkin' the same pavement as turncoat civvy guards.'

And so ended the affair with Jemmy McGurk going to the Barracks to explain the harmless little hoax that had put Armagh Jail on a red alert for six hours that day. On his release with a caution, Jemmy wiped his brow and took a vow that he would exercise great care in future dealings with the Holy Terror.

The Good Thief

The Governor of the prison and Oiney did not take the least bit kindly to each other, and when 'Shankill' opened the office door to march the Creevan lad in front of this very august Mr Purdy, the latter greeted the southern Irishman with a deep growl: 'Who told you to sit? Stand in front of the desk to attention! And stop gazing around!'

Oiney was truly astonished at the contents of the office; it resembled a warehouse. Only the desk where the heavy-jowled giant sat carried any appearance of clerical activities. Piled around the room was the most varied collection of garments and goods that Oiney had ever seen. There were boxes of shirts, bundles of stockings and knitwear, cartons of sweets, tins of groceries, pears, peaches and pineapples. Dozens of separate items lay scattered around on the floor and on chairs while the window ledge was heaped with a colourful assortment of gaudy ties.

'You're very popular around here,' said Mr Purdy with heavy sarcasm. 'Especially in Newry. Your published doggerel has touched the heartstrings of an easily moved populace. Gifts are pouring in. But tell me this! Why should a rascal like you be favoured more than the starving children of Africa and Asia? Answer me that!'

'I really don't know, mister, but you can have the lot for yourself if you just let me go back home to me granny in Creevan.'

The Governor gave a loud snigger that was immediately taken up by 'Shankill' who almost doubled up with great guffaws of mockery. 'Go back to your granny in Creevan? That'll be the day. That old headbanger that sent a dud battery to blow me up along with ill-wishes for me and my relations. Send you home to her? Are you joking? No fear. You just keep on writing your sob story and let the gifts pour in. But warn your friends! No more stupid gifts like files and hacksaw blades, or skeleton keys. One idiot even sent you in a rope-ladder. We only accept edible goods, clothes, books and the like. And what a bazaar and jumble sale we'll have in the local Orange Hall . . .'

'I do hope it's a success on behalf of the poor children of Africa and Asia,' said the generous Oiney.

'Africa and Asia my foot,' said Mr Purdy with a howl of laughter. 'Charity begins at home. On behalf of the Prison Staff's Benevolent Fund, a very important cause for warders' widows and orphans. Just you keep up the good work and we'll attend to your needs. We'll not kill the goose that lays the golden egg, shall we?'

'Are you calling me a goose, sir?' asked Oiney belligerently.

'Listen, sonny, I'm being nice to you, so just keep that effen trap of yours shut, do you hear! When you appear in Court in our own good time, we want no rag-and-bones man, so we'll have to fatten you up. We want no ugly comments from foreign observers who have recently come out of the woodwork. Constructive criticism – yes: adverse criticism – no! That's why I sent for you. It's the Prison Infirmary for you next week . . .'

'But I don't want to go there,' protested Oiney remembering that 'Abandon Hope' signboard mentioned by Mr Wayne.

'You'll go where we put you,' roared the Governor standing up, 'and that's final.'

According to Mr Wayne, the head of Armagh Jail was really a moderate man politically, totally dedicated to the abolition of the death sentence and flogging except in instances where prison governors and warders or their wives and families, relations and friends were the victims. As a boy he had been a keen ornithologist, risking his neck even in climbing the highest trees in his nest hunting and egg collecting, thus relieving many of our feathered friends of the dreadful anxiety and frenzied activity of bringing up their young. Apprenticed in an abbatoir, vulgarly called a slaughterhouse, he shunned the gory scenes as much as possible and advocated animal rights, strenuously demanding quicker means of disposing with the creatures. Like the good Customs Officer, he had graduated to Government service and high position through his lifelong, loving friendship with a dear friend in Stormont.

When Oiney returned to his cell with a woebegone expression on his pale face, he was astonished to find a two-tier bunk there instead of his low bed, and standing beside it a small, lean, agile fellow with a chirpy, cheeky face. This stranger, without introduction, kept winking at him and screwing the side of his face so frequently that Oiney wondered if the poor fellow had a permanent tic. He was beginning to feel quite sorry for him and was about to enquire after his health, but his kindly solicitude was quietly circumvented when the winking newcomer drew him down to a sitting position at the rear of the cell door out of 'Shankill's gaze. 'Don't worry about me, Oiney! I know all about you. Don't worry, I'm not a grass!'

Oiney's brows furrowed. A grass what, he felt like asking; he had never heard a sentence so incomplete. A grass widow? A grass lawn? A grass cricket or a grass market? Never just a grass! The more he lived in the world the stranger it grew.

Though he now sat close to the stranger, the latter still kept winking at him. 'Don't worry about me, pal! I'm Bobby Brown from the Falls ... D'you twig? I'm married to a Pape. The Falls, Pape, d'you twig? I got into your cell on pretence I'd get you to spill the beans an' then grass on you. No bloody fear. They've another guess comin'. Me name's Bobby Brown, Oiney. I'm on your side. Shake!'

Oiney's eternal glow of friendship for suffering humanity made him grasp the extended hand warmly. 'What are you in for, Bobby?' he asked with a sudden interest in the origin and statistics of the growing crime rate.

'Church an' chapel collection boxes Oiney.'

'Oh, I see. You're a charity worker then?'

'Are you joking? I pinch them. I can't stand churches and chapels ...'

59

'Well, if I was you Bobby,' said Oiney trying to be helpful, 'I'd just keep out o' them and avoid collection boxes.'

The stranger eyed him closely to see if he was serious. 'God knows you're the peculiar genius, Oiney, but never mind! I'm here to help spring you!'

A puzzled look came over the Creevan lad's face again: 'Spring me? What's that?'

'Help you escape, you nut. You're being transferred to the Infirmary block on Tuesday. We have a plant in the office . . .'

'Well,' said the confused Oiney, 'if you have a plant in the office I never seen it and I was there five minits ago. I seen ties an' shirts but not a flower-pot or plant . . .'

'A plant, an informer, you daft rookie. One who tells us the score. You're to be transferred on Tuesday and at ten past ten o'clock sharp that night you are to be on the flat roof of the Infirmary, via a trap-door in the ceiling of the linen room. One of the patients'll be there to guide you. Squeeze yourself through the trap-door an' close it tight behind you. Then hide behind the brick chimney an' wait the helicopter . . .'

'The what?' said the amazed and disbelieving Oiney.

'The helicopter. The great iron bird that's comin' to rescue you.'

'You're coddin' me now! Who'd want to rescue the likes o' me? In a helicopter as well! You're at the coddin' surely . . .'

'Cross me heart, Oiney! Why else would I come here an' tell you all this? You're far more important to the bhoys outside than you imagine. Especially since that article in the Newry paper. Their hearts bleed for you, Oiney. Is it all right, pal? Ten past ten sharp on Tuesday. Shake hands on it, Oiney.'

Oiney shook the stranger's hand although he still felt a bit dubious. Yet the more he thought he began to realise that almost equally strange things had happened to him in life. And that wink and twitch on Bobby's face was so completely disarming!

His excitement mounted as Tuesday drew nearer. His

spirits soared at even the faint hope of getting back to Creevan. Once there if anyone pursued him he knew lots of secret haunts among the high reeds and ferns around the lough and among the trees of Knockmaddy Woods. His mind was so alert with this pleasant prospect that he found it impossible to sleep, so he took advantage of his companion's eagerness to recount tales, exciting tales of his past life, all to pass the weary waiting hours.

'Why, Bobby,' he asked one night. 'Why demean your nice character by resortin' to pinchin' out of holy places?'

'Thank you, Oiney, I've not looked on it that way before. I've a totally unchristian regard for things sacred. I mean what really have I against the good Churches? After all what have they done to deserve my relievin' them of some o' their riches? Other than Inquisitions, fanaticism, sellin' Indulgences, banner blessing for wars an' Imperial stoogery an' several other similar trivial blemishes, our Churches have a history of absolute perfection, Piety personified. Mind you, Oiney, come to think of it, my resentment may come from some strange childhood experiences. It's possible, I think, yes, just possible . . .'

Oiney nodded his head in agreement. 'Mr Wayne the psychiatrist says everything can be explained that way . . .'

'That bonehead would, wouldn't he? But since you ask, Oiney, I'll give you me story to pass the time.'

They sat together on the bottom bunk and once again Oiney got lost in the strange experiences of another mortal on our little planet.

'I was born in Carrickfergus,' said Bobby, 'of Scottish-Irish descent. Me mother Millie was Irish an' me father George a good, dacint dour Scot. He was a docker to trade, an' me mother before she married an' had me, was a mill girl in West Belfast. Although she was a Pape an' he a Proddy, they got on great an' brought me up to the age of seven without bigotry of any kind. Then, Oiney, when I was seven, a terrible accident occurred to them on holiday at Glenarm when the bus overturned, and in one night in August I lost both of them. I was taken to an orphanage outside Belfast where I stayed for three years, and I tell you honestly, Oiney, I didn't like it one wee bit. In some ways the days o' Dickens haven't changed that much.

'But there was never a lad so happy when at the age of eleven I was adopted by the Reverend Cyril Brown and his grand missus Ethel, whose surname I still bear. They had a church mansion near Glengormley overlooking Belfast Lough an' not far from the Zoo. I spent the nicest days you could imagine in that ivy-clad house, and in the summer they took me everywhere around the glens of Antrim and up to the Giant's Causeway in the north an' the Long Man's grave an' God only knows where else. Me foster mother was a great charity worker at the Belfast docks an' there was nothin' the Reverend Brown liked to do better than read me extracts from the Good Book on the fine verandah of that house on a Sunday or quote poems from Milton an' *Paradise Lost* . . . I often thought since on the name *Paradise Lost*, it seemed surely to have an omen in it. They sent me to Portora boarding school down by the Border country where Oscar Wilde himself attended many years ago, but I didn't last there very long when the scandal broke out, not at the school Oiney, but at home. It was the same year as that other debacle took place when some minister ran away with the funds of the Orange Order across the water, but me foster father, thank God, wasn't involved in anythin' of that sort. He just, Oiney, had these wee sins o' the flesh, incidental wee longings an' cravings that grew insurmountable an' were looked on with great disdain in those puritan parts of Ulster.

'I was on me summer holiday from Portora when one Sunday he took me up to his study at Glengormley – Ethel was out at the time – to teach me the rudiments of elementary sex education which every good Christian father imparts to his son or should do. I knew, of course, a little about the subject from me days at Portora, but not nearly as much as me mentor. He drew references from the Bible on the theme an' honest to God, Oiney, I never saw a man wax so eloquent . . . After a while of divine exhortation the sweat ran down his forehead an' cheeks, his eyes danced out of his sockets an' honest to Christ, Oiney, he just couldn't stop himself. I never in me life saw a man in such a fit of pious enthusiasm, he got worked up to the limits. Unfortunately, a maid notorious for her prattlin' tongue saw the pair of us, an' the evil word spread around the Parish. Later when the discerning public learned that the good minister, not wishin' to confine these exalted lessons to the puny precincts of his home but extend them in the spirit of Christian charity to the choirboys of Whiteabbey, a number of outraged parents banded together to pour cold water on his rampant enthusiasm. As a result, Oiney, he was lodged in confinement in a special wing of Crumlin Jail and I was taken from me lovely ivy-clad home to a Boys' Home on the Ormeau Road in Belfast, where I continued me sex education although not on such a high plane. In that Home, I learned more than mere sex. I learned some of the finer points of knavery from young bedevilled outcasts of housing-schemes and inner city slums . . . A sex scandal broke out there as well but not with the same lofty religious overtones. It was not long before I graduated for Borstal training. There I learned to admire the skills of deception that ensure survival, for the most popular heroes among us were assuredly not the penitents or the goodly but the wily an' fearless. Yet for all the cynicism abroad, I still retained me humanity an' certain principles learned perhaps from the Good Book in those Sunday lessons given by me foster parent in his less rampant days.

'Eventually on my release from Borstal, after a long wait, I obtained work as a cross-ferry steward on the boat that was plyin' between Larne an' Stranraer. There I was able, after pickin' up a little experience, of puttin' me generous principles into practice. The hold of that ferry at the time was often crammed with poor emigrants and equally poor farm-servants comin' an' going from their homes in Ireland. Very few o' them could afford the full price of a comfortable cabin midship, so when the boat was on its way an' most of the crew asleep, I devised the most kind, humane plan possible, Oiney. I had them transferred to these comfortable bunks at quarter the official price, an amount which I pocketed, not merely with a clear conscience but a sense of great pride. For I wasn't even diddlin' the Company. Wouldn't the cabins be otherwise empty?

'I continued in this noble and charitable enterprise for a number of years until I was shopped by an envious workmate, inspired no doubt, by the Evil One, an' thus terminated my mission o' mercy. Such is life, Oiney, so no matter how high or noble your aspirations, beware o' the snake in the grass. I was forced then in leaner times to work as an assistant stall hand in the Smithfield Market in Belfast, near Castle Junction, the city centre. It was at Smithfield with its stalls an' books an' records and a teemin' market that I decided to improve me livelihood. You see it was at this time I met me future wife Jenny, a bonny girl from the Antrim Road in Belfast, an' though we had a different background I knew she was the one for me. I didn't need to change me religion nor she hers, for we didn't make it an issue. We got a place in the Lower Falls an' funny enough, it wasn't long before I began to see their point o' view. It wasn't a religious thing, just nationality an' common sense. There were, I know, Oiney, far brighter Proddies than me came round to that decision before I was born even. Well, be that as it may, I found it hard enough to make ends meet at Smithfield so I hit on this plan o' hawkin' holy pictures around Ireland . . .'

'You did not!' exclaimed the astonished Oiney. 'Surely to God, a Protestant wouldn't sell Catholic pictures around holy Ireland?'

'Me hand up to God I did that very thing, an' for a long, long time made a very good livin' out of it too. I'm not boastin' Oiney, but I sold them holy pictures like hot cakes outside the chapels at Mission times and at country markets an' fairs. I'm a broadminded chap an' wasn't I servin' the masses like I did on that damn boat? I'll tell you this too, Oiney. The poor of Ireland were me best customers be far, for havin' little or nothin' on this earth aren't they lookin' for a seat o' comfort in the next. D'you twig, Oiney?' He gave one of his familiar, roguish winks.

'Tell me this, Bobby,' said Oiney. 'Did you not make enough money at the pictures to keep you clear o' dippin' in the offertory collection boxes?'

'Listen, Oiney,' explained Bobby. 'It's all a question o' Market Economy. Yes, that's what it is.'

'What's Market Economy?' asked the open-mouthed Oiney.

'It's like this. Supply and Demand, Oiney. That's how it works. Let me explain. In the average household goods there's always a quick turnover. Bread, butter, cheese an' milk are consumed nearly as quickly as they're produced. Even pots an' pans, brushes an' what have you get knocked about an' need replacin'. But holy pictures, Oiney! Now they're a different kettle o' fish. They hang up on the wall away from children's reach, an' sad to say, remain there a permanent feature. Only an earthquake, a landslide, or artillery fire can shift them. After the first sale, unfortunately they last as long, an' sometimes longer, than the house itself. They survive pestilence an' plague an' hail, rain an' snow; they hang up there despite cursin', shoutin' an' drunken revelry an' even auction sales. So you see, Oiney lad, the market's limited, and in these wretched circumstances, what can a poor man resort to but unorthodox ways o' gettin' a livin'? But think, Oiney, if you have any qualms o' conscience, think of all the gold pillaged by our good Churches from Aztecs, Incas an' the like in soul-savin missions. They can't preach morality, can they?'

'What are these Inkas and Asticks you're talkin' about, Bobby?'

'Oh, go to sleep, Oiney, an' get ready for the high jump on Tuesday. I only wish to God I was goin' with you.'

Oiney did not sleep too well that night. He lay awake a long time thinking of the wild adventures of that strange companion lying in the bunk above him. What an incredible world surely we were all born into, with myriads of folk whose rich or sad lives are intertwined with ours yet often so far apart. Outside Armagh jail, the wind was rising and blowing, blowing over Creevan among the rushes and sedges of the rippling lough, a peaceful, simple scene that he hoped to soon enjoy away from this tumult.

Escape

A bitter cold evening it was as Oiney huddled close to the warm chimney on the roof of the jail Infirmary. No one, he felt certain, had observed his departure from the ward to the toilet and thence into the linen closet. He was clad only in pyjamas and he now scanned the darkening skies for any sign of his rescuers. He could see the lights of the ancient city of Armagh all around him, and away to the east rose the deep dark contour of part of the Mourne mountain range. To the south lay Creevan, his native village. Soon perhaps he would be walking its quiet, homely streets and telling his pal Jonjo the terrible things which can befall a man for just being decent and kind.

His granny, of course, would rant and rave at him and call him everything under the sun for not fetching home the little brown jug. She would tell him once again that he could not put a foot across the threshold without causing some awful calamity. And indeed, Oiney was beginning to believe that there was more than a grain of truth in what she said about him. With this fearful thought in mind, he left the comfort of the chimney to haul a heavy beam of wood across the roof in order to block access from the more frail trap-door.

At last, to his great relief, he heard the loud purring noise of the large helicopter as it circled to land on the roof which it lit first with a powerful beam. A door opened on its side and a muffled masked figure ran towards him. 'Quick, Oiney, quick! Get aboard!'

He recognised that voice and immediately he recoiled. There was no mistaking the rich twang of the Dublin back-streets.

'Oh no, Shaun! You're not on! You're just not on! I've had more than enough of you and that failed priest. I want nothin' to do with the pair of you. I'll even endure the antics of an eccentric psychiatrist and the greed of a grotesque Governor before I'll forgive the perfidy of a false friend.'

'Begod, Oiney, them's powerful words, powerful words indeed. But when you hear my story, you'll surely understand that we didn't betray you . . .'

'Tell all that to the marines,' said Oiney indignantly. 'Doyle's son, indeed! An' the deranged hermit. I suppose his hut didn't take off that night?'

'An' did you not find the Customs Officer a bit of a screwball yourself, Oiney? I'm not goin' to argue with you on top of this roof all night, but I'm tellin' you honestly, the oul' rat Doyle did desert me mother an' me . . . I'll explain it all to you aboard . . .'

The others in the waiting helicopter seemed to be becoming impatient also, for Oiney saw a young woman in a dark green suit running towards him.

'This is Aileen,' said Shaun, 'an' believe me Oiney, she admires you immensely.' And as if to prove her friend correct, Aileen threw her arms around Oiney and hugged him tightly. 'You're my best hero Oiney, in the whole wide world.' She looked at him, those lovely hazel-brown eyes of hers glowing with worship. She had boyish, clear-cut features of firm resolve, an aspect that Oiney adored so much; she wore little silver ear-rings of a simple Celtic design, and her fair hair cut in something akin to a page-boy style had a reddish tinge. With those endearing arms around him she became to Oiney a delightful, warm vision of the heroic maiden of Erin. He did not know a single girl in Creevan or Carrick who could tread the same ground as her.

'Aileen works with props in the Abbey Theatre in Dublin,' Shaun explained, 'an' she's goin' to help us to disguise you. She belongs to the Movement.'

Oiney did not know what props or the Movement were, and to tell the truth he did not care as long as this brave girsha had her arms around him.

'Oh, I heard all about you Oiney,' she said, 'all about your Creevan adventures an' Lough Derg an' how you helped Shaun an' Sheamus over that Customs place. You'll go down into the history books for generations to come.'

Oiney had completely forgotten Shaun's presence until he heard an impatient, almost gruff exclamation, 'Aren't you pair comin' on board?'

Arm in arm with Aileen, Oiney, forgetful for the moment of his feud with Shaun, was thus inveigled aboard the craft, where the smiling Sheamus and a young pilot dressed in an American uniform sat ready for take-off.

Soon they were flying south over the border. Oiney sat looking down on the little hills and lakes of Monaghan in the moonlight. His head was quite dizzy, for this was his first time in an aircraft, and he shivered with the cold.

'Give the poor fella a flask o' tay an' a sandwich Aileen,' said Shaun, adding with a smile, 'We'll have something warmer for him to wear shortly, won't we, Aileen?'

Oiney turned to his erstwhile friend. The tea admittedly was hot and very refreshing, but Shaun had still some deep explaining to do before Oiney would ever trust him or Sheamus again. He looked at the Dublin man: 'You promised, Shaun, that you would clear matters up as soon as we boarded.'

'Ah yes,' agreed Shaun, 'so I did. Now where was I?'

'Doyle had deserted your Mum an' you. During your terrible years o' deprivation in the back-streets o' Dublin your mother became a single-minded Irish rebel, which without a shadow of a doubt won your deepest admiration. Isn't that right?'

'Begod,' said Sheamus admiringly, 'your erudition and elocution grows with the hour, Oiney. I knew from the beginnin' you had it in you.'

Although Oiney did not know the meaning of the big words used by Sheamus they sounded very favourable so he let them pass.

'Yes Oiney,' agreed Shaun, 'you've summarised me statement well. Me mother in Dublin at first became a very staunch rebel, enlistin' me in the Cause as well. An' then . . . an' then she did the most dastardly thing imaginable . . .'

His voice broke and Oiney had to encourage him: 'What did she do, Shaun?'

'I never knew she could descend so low . . .'

'What did she do, Shaun?'

'She married a civvy guard. That's what she did.'

Aileen shook her head and made a shuddering grimace. 'Wasn't that the most disgustin' thing to do Oiney?'

'If you say so, Aileen . . .'

'I haven't seen me mother from that day to this,' continued Shaun. 'I left me house in a stormin' rage an' I've never been back. Oiney, we cannot keep you in the dark any longer. You've probably guessed about Sheamus an'me already. Well, you can now add Aileen. We're dedicated to the Movement an' the Border hut had to go up that night.'

'But you didn't give me time for an Act of Contrition or the last wee puff of a cigarette. I wasn't even given time to shrive me most precious possession, me invisible soul.'

'We hadn't time for such niceties,' admitted Shaun, 'but we didn't intend you to stand gabbin' with that silly Customs man for so long. We waited for you at the bridge for quite a time an' then when the thing went off, we said a prayer for the repose of your soul. We knew that as a good innocent Catholic you'd go straight to Heaven. After the explosion, we wrote you off . . .'

'You what?' exclaimed the astounded Oiney, wondering had he heard right.

'But we did say a prayer for the repose of your immortal soul as I have said,' continued Shaun.

'Well that was kind of you, very kind of you indeed,' agreed Oiney.

'An' besides,' said the Dublin man, 'had you gone up with the hut that night, you would have died for the Cause.'

'But supposin',' said Oiney, 'just supposin' I didn't want to die for the Cause.'

'Have you not learned yet, Oiney, that for all our plans an' weary watchfulness, we still cannot be absolutely certain of our individual destinies? Some of the greatest heroes o' Mankind are still unsung. History sometimes raises fakes to temporary grandeur, creatures like Hitler, Mussolini an' Franco, while many a real hero goes to an unmarked grave, caught in the crossfire . . .'

Oiney tugged fiercely at Shaun's jacket.

'Shaun, quick, we're passin' the hills o' Carrick. Aren't we goin' to land near Creevan?'

'Our plans are somewhat different, Oiney. In the manetime listen while I conclude me story. After the hut went up, Sheamus an' I continued our journey to the shores of Lough Neagh, an' an American air-base where we had a friend workin' as the canteen manageress. She disposed of the booze for us at a fair price. And betther still we made friends with some American-Irish pilots at the base. All very well until we read your story. You were like a voice from the dead. Of course, but of course, we welcomed the good news that you had survived the blast. But, my God, that notebook of yours published in the Newry newspaper . . . It was heartrending. Sheamus an' I used to be in tears readin' it. Aileen there'll confirm it.'

'It's true, Oiney, as I'm sittin' here lookin' at me hero. I used to see them wipin' their eyes . . .'

'It had a big lump in me throat,' said Sheamus, 'a lump in me throat that hurts me still.'

'But by Christ, Oiney lad,' said Shaun, 'were you blabbin'! You were spillin' everythin'. They were obviously feedin' you on dope. You were talkin' like a budgie an' next thing you'd be givin' them our identities. Remember you were the only one saw us at that Border. We had to spring you from Armagh Jail. Luckily for us, we found the right man.'

Shaun pointed to the helicopter pilot.

'Wolfe T. Carey, a Brooklyn man whose father came from old Kildare. An' more genuine Irish than some o' your chancers who only concern themselves with savin' their skin in this world an' their cowardly souls in the next . . . Naw, Oiney, as much as we liked you, you had to be silenced. So we hit on this plan. Remember us tellin' you that Sheamus here is a failed priest. Well that's true. He went for a few years to Clunagh Monastery in Tipperary. It's a Cistercian Order an' they have this lovely vow of silence which suits our circumstances down to the ground. We intend to dhrop you there, an' you can wear this monastic garb which Aileen has kindly provided from the stage wardrobe. You can mingle, Oiney, with the good monks an' be one o' them. You can also adopt a monastic name like Sebastian, or Augustus, or Benedict . . . The other monks will not be able to question your presence; they'll probably think you have been transferred from Mount Melleray or England. And so for a year or two you can settle in silent piety until all this blows over. So try Oiney for size with the robe, Aileen!'

Oiney tried to make a last protest. 'But I haven't got this . . . this vocation thing that Sheamus was talkin' about in the van. I just haven't got it.'

'Never mind the vocation Oiney,' said Shaun, a bit gruffly. 'It's a vacation you need an' we'll see that you get it.'

Aileen attached a belt around Oiney's waist and then sat back to admire his new appearance. 'Mother o' God, don't you look lovely,' she said with unfeigned admiration, 'a shinin' saint of Heaven no less! Just a wee hair trim with the scissors an' you'd only want a halo. Aren't you the spittin' image of Saint Francis? I'll never forget you, Oiney,' she continued tearfully, 'an' I want you to remember me as well in your devotions an' prayers. An' when it all blows over, won't we meet again in far better times?'

Though the monk's habit was a great deal warmer than the pyjamas, Oiney sat somewhat mystified and shaken by the rapid turn of events. He had nothing against the Cistercians, of course, but he dreaded the vow of silence. There was nothing he loved in life better than a good chat. And those awful names Shaun had chosen. Why, Sebastian almost sounded vulgar. Benedict really smelt of the wine, while Augustus was so imperious and snobby. He had not much time, however, to browse over his fears, for the helicopter dropped lower and lower as it circled the monastery gardens. Fortunately for the intruders the church organ in the inner chapel drowned out the loud noise. The pilot signalled Shaun, who soon returned with some information.

'We cannot land, but Wolfe will dhrop you as close to the ground as makes no difference. He'll try an' find a space between the apple trees. Goodbye an', Oiney son, remember the Cause in your meditations!'

There were tears in Aileen's eyes, she hated partings so much, but Oiney had little time to study that sad face. Sheamus opened the door and a not too gentle push from Shaun had the Creevan lad falling into a new, a different life.

Brother Excelsis

The good Abbot of Clunagh Monastery had been for many years awaiting a most important manifestation from Heaven. Ancient legend, written in the monastery scrolls and preserved in the precious library, told how one day the saintly monk Brother Excelsis would one day be rewarded for his deep devotion and good deeds. He had, while living, asked the Lord to allow him to return from Heaven to earth some future day to assure the good monks of Clunagh that their sublime faith in the hereafter was really justified. According to Excelsis, Heaven had answered his unusual request in a most favourable manner, sending none other than that very jovial messenger Gabriel with the good news. Gabriel had told him that it was such an odd request that not a single saint in the litany of saints or the whole of Christendom had ever requested this simple but important favour of assuring their relatives and dear friends of Heaven's real existence, while answering for once and for all the sceptic's eternal snigger 'that no one has ever come back from the dead to tell us about the far side'.

Indeed the long delay in Excelsis's return had in itself caused quite a degree of irritability among the monks of Clunagh itself. Why, only last week, the good Abbot Father Boniface had to admonish Ignatius for stealing a print of butter from Brother Placid's plate in the refectory. The silly deed fitted more into college rather than monastic life. Placid's reprisal on the other hand was positively outrageous; he had emptied a full basin of water over Ignatius's cell. Brother Placid had always been a source of concern to Father Boniface, who was a ruddy, jovial and tolerant friar. It was the latter who had suggested the adoption by the novice of the name Placid, to remind the monk of the state of grace for which he should strive. Brother Placid constantly relapsed into fits of ill-temper during which he jumped up and down, rolled his eyes and rattled his teeth. Boniface was forever making apologies for Placid's outbursts, for the latter was in charge of the Monastery Guest House and had driven folk away ... folk who had merely sought a brief haven of peace and prayer in Clunagh.

One morning after a long night of prayer the devout Abbot was gazing dreamily at the rows of apple trees surrounding the monastery when suddenly a small brown object wriggling in a distant tree caught his attention. What on earth could it be? He crept quietly along the deserted corridor to Brother Andrew's cell; he was a young, eager monk in charge of the gardens.

'I think, Brother,' said the Abbot gently, so as not to awaken the other monks, 'I think we have an interloper.'

'Good heavens,' replied the startled Andrew, sitting up in bed and looking wildly around the cell. 'An interloper? Good Lord! Where?'

'In the orchard, on a distant tree. It's a dog or goat, perhaps. If so, it could ruin the fruit. Would you please investigate, Andrew?'

The Abbot crossed over to the window and looked out. 'Yes, it is still there, Brother.'

It was only a matter of minutes before the young monk returned to Father Boniface, all breathless and excited. 'It ... it ... it is no dog or goat, Father. It isn't, Father, it isn't.'

'Calm yourself, Brother! What is it then?'

'It's a monk, Father.'

'It cannot be. A monk?'

'It is one our brethren, Father, and yet not one of us.'

Father Boniface on previous occasions had had to reprimand Brother Andrew for speaking like a biblical text: 'I have told you before, Andrew, not to speak in riddles or divers tongues. What do you mean by "not one of us"? Summon all the lay-brethren!'

Brother Andrew knocked on the cell doors and soon all the brown-robed lay-monks were assembled in the long corridor. Brother Placid was especially grumpy at being aroused from his deep slumber, and few of the yawning brethren indeed looked jubilant. They lined up silently while the Abbot counted them. Thirty-five in all. Correct. He made a careful recount. But the total came to the same. They were all there to a man. Then where in God's name did the strange monk come from? It seemed so inexplicable.

Then suddenly the wondrous flash of divine inspiration shone through the heavy, hard stone walls of Clunagh and sent the good Father Boniface to his knees, chanting: 'Venite adoramus! Glory to the Lord on High! Our prayers have been answered. It can only be the saintly Excelsis. He has arrived at last.'

Some cynics and sceptics (atheists, no doubt) may criticise Heaven's poor marksmanship that landed the saint in an apple tree, but when we consider the incredible journey the good Excelsis had made from paradise across the star-studded universe without colliding with a star, asteroid or comet, when we consider the saint's safe landing on planet Earth even, not to mention a little island called Ireland in the vast Atlantic it is feat enough to astonish the average person. To land the good monk intact and still breathing in a targeted monastery garden, albeit in an apple tree, is so utterly beyond human comprehension that it deserves to be classified and locked away forever as one of the great mysteries of Faith. The Abbot had every cause indeed for great jubilation, and Heaven equally so for its almost perfect aim.

The monks, now guided by Boniface and augmented by the white-robed priests, all gathered around the apple tree in which poor Oiney, facing downward, was lodged. The entire monastery community was present. The brown, the snow-white habits, the rosy ripe apples, the green leaves, the man cleft in the branches, all contrived to make a quaint scene

75

reminiscent of some out-of-the-way mediaeval canvas. The good Abbot went on his knees under the tree and extended his arms: 'Welcome, Brother Excelsis! A hundred thousand welcomes on your return to Clunagh Monastery!'

And just in case the Gaelic language was more likely than not spoken in Clunagh hundreds of years ago, Boniface made it his business to convey his message in that language also, a custom which has been kindly extended ever since to foreign visitors.

The open, honest, bewildered and extremely innocent face of Oiney, and his prison pallor, added to by the chill of the early morning air, gave him such an unearthly glow that no one in his senses could possibly doubt his heavenly origin. Two agile monks climbed up the tree and by releasing the saint brought the divine mission to a perfect conclusion. Oiney now stood on his feet in the garden where Boniface embrace him warmly: 'Now that you have finally arrived, good Excelsis, I pray you, favour us with your heavenly blessing.'

Oiney had no trouble whatsoever in giving this small service. After the misery of that jail in Armagh and the inhuman treatment of vile screws like Shankill and the Governor, the warmth of welcome in this monastery garden sent a rich glow of gratitude through his body and he could truthfully exclaim, with tears in his eyes, 'I bless the hour God sent me among you, for Heaven knows it's great to be away from that jail and Shaun an' Sheamus even with all their dirty conniving . . . God knows I really like the lot o' you already, and I think that next to Heaven this is the best possible place I could be in the wide world. I give you all me blessings surely.'

The monks received this short speech favourably though with silent applause, the latter being the only kind permissible in Clunagh. At first they wondered at the strange references to Shaun and Sheamus by Excelsis, but concluded that the saint's collision with the apple tree had caused slight concussion, a better excuse than most for rambling.

'I will bring you to my cell,' said the Abbot, 'for surely, Excelsis, you must be tired and hungry after such a long journey.'

76

As they walked towards the monastery, Oiney could not help thinking that Shaun and Sheamus had really picked the perfect haven for him. For all his mishaps, what incredible good luck followed his path occasionally. He could not, of course, for the life of him understand the almost slavish adulation of these good monks, but Heaven knows, it was a welcome relief to a poor Creevan nonentity who had only known in the main snobbery, poverty and abuse. Even the name they had chosen for him, Excelsis, carried a sweet, unusual poetry in its very sound.

The Abbot, to be quite fair and honest, had another more prosaic reason for inviting Oiney to a repast in the quiet of his cell. He had this consuming desire to know all about Heaven. Even a desire quite stronger than that. To know all about Heaven before anyone else in the world. Just this one small failing marred the perfection that was Father Boniface. Knowing too the old maxim that no man but a liar likes to talk on an empty stomach, the Abbot had several courses of fish and vegetables placed before Excelsis. He was not prepared, however, to witness the speed with which the holy saint demolished each plateful: 'Holy Moses,' gasped Boniface. 'Don't they feed you up there? Didn't you have somethin' to ate before you came down? Nectar or ambrosia, perhaps?'

Oiney screwed up his nose. 'Nectar, ambrosia me eye! Feed you, did you say? Sure, I only had a flask o' tay an' a few sandwiches in all the time I was up there. I was starvin' . . .'

'Excelsis, I beg you. Tell me what it is really like up there?'

'I'll tell you this, Father. It's shockin' cold up there. If you ever think o' goin' up there, Father, you betther wear flannel drawers an' a fur coat.'

'My God,' gasped the Abbot, rapidly becoming disillusioned and desperately grasping for any little measure of merit left. 'But surely, surely, Excelsis, you were happy up there in the company o' the saints?'

Oiney gazed at Boniface, wondering if he was in his right mind. 'Happy up there in the company o' saints? Are you jokin', Father? Saints did you call them? Smugglers, Father, conspirators, Father, revolutionaries an' reds, Father! That's what they are.'

The good Abbot sank on his knees. 'Oh, my God! My God! Have they taken over up there as well?'

The Guest

During the first weeks which followed Oiney's miraculous and sudden descent from the clouds the Abbot of Clunagh was forced to conclude that Oiney had never been to Heaven at all but instead to some draughty, cold region up there populated by radicals and fiery dissidents. The low temperature and location ruled out Hell. It now seemed certain to Boniface that Excelsis the mediaeval monk had been confined, for reasons best known to the Creator, to a draughty corridor somewhere near Purgatory. In all probability he had fallen through a hole, causing the draught. The recent scientific speculation about black empty pockets in the universe gave the Abbot's theory a certain plausability. The good man was also deeply concerned with some of the 'saint's' most outrageous statements about Heaven and, afraid that these might filter through to monks of lesser conviction, thought it in the interests of everyone to have the newcomer transferred to the Monastery Guest House, where he could labour under the watchful eye of the ill-tempered Brother Placid.

This Guest House was a whitish-grey turreted building just outside the monastery proper. It had the appearance more of a grandiose stage-set than a real edifice, but it had for decades been the comfortable living-quarters of people visiting Clunagh on Retreat. Others came on short periods of 'cure' for the excessive imbibing of wine or spirits. The third main category of Guest House residents were past pupils of the adjacent College returning either on nostalgic trips to scenes of boyhood glory or to participate in the annual rugby match against the current Seniors. It was, of course, considered a great honour to be invited to play against the Alma Mater.

Brother Placid saw in Excelsis a certain unworldliness of which even the most pious would be inclined to take advantage. Oiney on the other hand saw in Placid's eyes a nervous, jittery glint that predicted sudden sharp explosions. Here was a holy man one had to treat with caution.

'Your duties here will be quite simple,' said Placid in a sing-song voice he had acquired in years of chanting during the canonical hours of Matins, Nocturne and the others. His post as Guest House supervisor had given him the freedom of normal speech for only the second time in years, but as he had quite forgotten the ordinary cadences of speech he sang his phrases instead. All this bewildered Oiney at first; then it amused him, so much so that when left on his own, which was quite often, he would mimic Placid's chanting voice.

'Don't forget . . . omnia vincit labor . . . dearest Brother . . . put some coal . . . on the fire . . . Amen.'

That first day at the Guest House his voice had intoned a long list of Oiney's new duties: 'You will make the beds . . . lay the fires . . . sweep the rooms . . . prepare the breakfasts . . . lay the tables . . . serve the tables . . . wash the dishes . . . clean the brasses . . . carry the luggage . . .'

'And in me spare time in between . . .' asked Oiney reeling under the never-ending litany. Apart from patience, however, the other great ingredient missing from Placid's character was a sense of humour.

He merely gave Oiney a sharp look: 'You will mow the lawn . . . and clip the hedges.'

Oiney considered asking him were there no plumbing or painting jobs but he wisely considered it safer to maintain his vow of silence in this strange fellow's company.

Placid's contribution to running the Guest House, during Oiney's term of office at least, was to sit on a broad stool in a small souvenir kiosk at the base of one of the towers facing the route to and from the main public church. Even in his very first week the Creevan lad caught a glimpse of his superior's nasty temper when the monastery cat, Batty, knocked the milk jug over a bundle of holy tracts. The irate monk swore at it in Latin, at least that is what Oiney thought; then Placid took off his sandals and slung them after the frightened, fleeing animal. The next instant he was on his knees imploring Heaven's forgiveness.

Oiney helped the penitent to his feet and began to advise him how to look on the bright side, and keep right on to the end of the road, in fact, the very same lecture he had recently read to the strange psychiatrist in Armagh. Suddenly to his deep dismay a large bible flung by Placid glanced off the side of his head. The monk had again risen from his stool, and was shouting angrily: 'You gibberin' gabbin chatterbox, d'you ever keep that gob o' yours shut? Whatever made you join an Order of silent monks, for you're the least suited to monastic life, of all the people I ever met! You should have found yourself a job in the subway or the tower o' Babel, where the masses congregate . . .'

Oiney nursed the bump on his head and his grievance for a few days and then forgot about both of them. It was not in his nature to harbour ill-will against the likes of Placid, who was obviously the tragic victim of some youthful mishap. The Guest House duties absorbed his own complete attention. He found the cooking to be the most strenuous, for he knew absolutely nothing about it. He had never even boiled an egg in his lifetime. For this reason the food he served sent many of the guests packing and others into hospital with dysentry and diarrhoea which, of course, eased his task considerably.

In his very occasional spare time he explored first of all the Guest House itself and then the spacious grounds of the large lay college belonging to the monastery. In the lost property room of the Guest House he saw an amazing collection of discarded or forgotten articles; among these were twelve umbrellas, a bird-cage, a Gladstone bag, a leather-bound whiskey flask, a sword, a small cannon, a suit of clothes, a pack of cards, a racing gambler's calendar, a miniature china copy of the Taj Mahal, an elephant's tusk and a teapot.   .

His visits through the College grounds brought even greater surprises. For an academy with a mere two or three hundred boarders and no day-boys the sports facilities were quite astonishing. There were six football pitches, three tennis courts with additional ones made up in the summer, two handball alleys, a miniature golf course and a grand pavilion. Back in Creevan he and pals had to put up with a small patch of ground and Oiney had seen the adult team play on a partially waterlogged meadow. None of the college boys ever ran these roads and lanes barefoot. Instead they were all dressed like young gentlemen of Eton and Harrow and strode through Clunagh grounds with a lofty hauteur. They passed Oiney on the pathway without as much as a quick glance of curiosity. This was an Ireland unknown to him, and every bit as strange to him as the paradise of Boniface.

Although most visitors to Clunagh Guest House paid little or no attention to Oiney, one day there arrived a gentleman who took exceptional and somewhat unwelcome interest in his activities. Shortly after the arrival of this inquisitive guest, Brother Placid, panting and puffing, called Oiney into the souvenir shop.

'Oh, dear me, Excelsis, I see the great man himself has arrived . . .'

'Great man? Now who would he be, Brother?'

'P.P. O'Reilly.'

'I'm sorry, Brother, but I never heard of him.'

'Oh, my dear Excelsis, your education has been sadly neglected then. Treat the man graciously, for P.P. O'Reilly almost died for Ireland durin' the Troubles . . .'

'Almost died for Ireland . . .'

'Yes, the Flying Column car he was in drove over the jetty in Cork harbour. The other three were drowned but P.P. was hauled ashore. Run immediately, Excelsis, an' tell the College superior that P.P. is here to see his son Luke! Take the boy back with you to the Guest House! Do hurry, Excelsis!'

Luke O'Reilly was a tall, rather frail-looking aesthete of fifteen or sixteen years. He wore gold-rimmed spectacles and had already acquired the habit from Father Francis of peering over the top of them. He was a great reader and Oiney saw a book jutting out of his blazer pocket. 'Is that a class-book?' he asked.

'Indeed no,' Luke replied, drawing the book from his pocket. 'I only wish it was. *My Fight for Irish Freedom* by Dan Breen a class-book? That'll be the day. Brother! Some of the teachers here would burn Dan Breen at the stake. They were in O'Duffy's Blueshirts . . .'

'Don't you like the College, Luke?'

'One or two of the teachers are all right. The rest are a rummy crew. Most o' the boys are snooty-nosed brats . . . The scholarship lads who won their way here are fine. One is my best pal. The rest of the pupils are the spoilt sons of big farmers and publicans . . . No, I don't like Clunagh College and I never will. Has my father been here long?'

'No, he is only just arrived. Brother Placid says he's a great man.'

'Duck's Belly would say that, wouldn't he?'

'Duck's Belly?' said the puzzled Oiney.

'Yes. that's what we used to call Placid when he taught Latin. And what a wicked-tempered brute he was if we forgot our declensions! He used to murder us. We used to ask him to translate silly phrases like "The leader of the war knows already". *Dux belli scit jam.* Duck's belly shit jam. See!' Luke O'Reilly burst into hilarious schoolboyish laughter that was such a contrast to his usual fairly morose self.

'My father is anything but a great man. He merely thinks he is. Most of the great men were shot, imprisoned or hounded out of Ireland.

'I hate it when my Da comes down to Clunagh. I just hate it. He brags and boasts about what he did for Ireland, and admiring clowns like Placid lead him on and encourage him. I haven't seen you before. What's your name?'

'Brother Excelsis. I haven't been here long.'

Luke gave him a quick, yet amused look.

83

'Say, aren't you the chap that's supposed to have arrived recently from Heaven? One of the teaching monks let it out and now the whole college is talking about it. You see there was this legend . . .' Luke O'Reilly went on to explain and for the first time, the whole affair became crystal clear to Oiney. Imagine mistaking him for a saint! For an instant he considered going to the Abbot and confessing that he had been dropped from an helicopter, but the very serious consequences which would arise from such an admission horrified him. He was wearing his monk's habit and masquerading as a Cistercian lay-brother. And, even if he told the absolute truth, who would give any credence to such an unlikely story? Dropped from a helicopter and dressed up like a monk? What utter nonsense! Oiney assured the smiling Luke that he was by no means a saint and wisely left it at that.

The man who almost died for Ireland stayed at the Guest House for three days, and whenever Oiney swept the great man's rooms he was certain that he detected quite a pungent aroma reminiscent of Doyle's parlour on the night of the Wake. Then in the dining-room, he began to notice that O'Reilly was observing him very closely. Even as Oiney polished the wall mirror there was always the horrible reflection of this heavy-jowled creature staring at him with a bemused look on his flushed and ugly countenance.

On the morning of his departure, O'Reilly called Oiney over to his table. He pointed to an empty chair opposite him. 'Sit down!'

Oiney sat down.

'Brother Excelsis?'

'Yes?'

P.P. O'Reilly gave a great guffaw of disbelief: 'Don't make me laugh! Saint Excelsis! The monks here think you're a bloody saint.' He caught hold of Oiney's robe and twisted part of it in his large fist. 'Well I know you're no saint. Why? Because in the first instance you haven't got a halo! Every saint worth his salt has got a halo. Tell me, just you tell me!

Have you ever in your life seen a picture of a saint without a halo? Have you?'

Oiney had to admit that what Mr P.P. O'Reilly said was gospel truth.

'There you are,' said the great man. 'And another thing. What bloody saint looks at himself in the mirror all day? Tell me that!'

Oiney did not wish to inform his questioner that he was merely keeping an eye on P.P. himself.

'A saint doesn't puff himself up with pride and vanity,' continued O'Reilly, a great authority on the behaviour of saints. 'A saint has humility and self-negation. A saint walks with his halo on his lonely road with a simple dignity that marks him out to be a . . . a . . .'

'Saint,' suggested Oiney helpfully.

The man who almost died for Ireland looked Oiney straight in the eyes and the Creevan lad knew for certain the game was up. O'Reilly's gaze was a cold, hard one. 'I don't even believe you're a real monk. Listen lad! I haven't been a Superintendent of the Irish Civic Guards for thirty years for nothing. I've a photographic memory. You have heard of James Joyce, haven't you? Well, I can recite *Finnegans Wake* from "riverrun past Eve's and Adam's" till its last unfinished circular sentence! And I've summed you up. Not long ago, there was this country yokel from Creevan by the name of Oiney Hoy who made an incredible escape by helicopter from the roof of Armagh Jail . . . The earth seemed to have opened and swallowed you up. But you were here all the time posin' as a saint . . . What a disguise!'

'I never said I was a saint,' Oiney protested feebly. 'And what are you goin' to do? Have me arrested again?'

'Not a bit of it,' said O'Reilly, ' so don't panic! Everything will be all right if you agree to my plan. I've watched you for days. An' when you're not lookin' in the bloody mirror you can graft. I must admit, you can certainly graft. Not a word to Placid or anyone else if you do as I say. I own a small, select place near Killiney, south of Dublin . . . a kind of unusual hotel . . . We cater for folk from the great Art world . . . Art and Literature . . . Now I need a new general factotum. And apart from your cooking, which God knows is abominable, you'd suit me fine. In return I'll keep your secret and pay you a few bob a week and your keep. How's that? Killiney's a fine place by the sea and you can always say you walked in the footsteps of James Joyce.'

Oiney saw that there was little chance of escape from the cunning net which O'Reilly had cast. On this occasion he would play for time: he did not relish being under the great man's roof. 'You'll have to bring me some suitable clothes, Mr O'Reilly. I can hardly do hotel work in this outfit.'

The hotel owner gave him a little card and some money. 'So it's agreed, then. I'll be down on Saturday morning with some clothes. Mind you, I'm keeping you to your word and woe betide you if . . .'

The situation was desperate. Oiney could only pray that some miracle would save him. He tried to be more pleasant to Brother Placid should the worst happen and O'Reilly reveal the truth. 'I understand, Brother Placid,' he said next morning, 'that you are a very holy man in spite of little minor lapses of temper.'

'Good heavens, no,' exclaimed Placid. 'If you want real holiness you would need to visit my cousin, Pat McNulty, in the village of Roshinne. Now there's a pious fellow for you. Pat's the boy for you. I hear rumours even of his miraculous powers. Ah, that's what I'd call sanctity galore.'

Later that day while Oiney was cleaning P.P. O'Reilly's vacated room, he discovered a discarded whiskey bottle in a drawer of the press. He was about to dispose of it in the open rubbish bin when he heard the low sing-song voice of Placid coming from the corridor.

'Rinse it in the sink . . . Remove the label . . . Wrap the object in an old newspaper . . . Everyone of us has our little failings . . . Even the great . . . *Humanum est errare* . . . To err is human.'

Oiney was so taken aback by the rapid succession of strange events that he decided to take a quiet stroll that evening by the pleasant banks of a little stream which flowed down the green fields at the rear of the Guest House. He had walked about a quarter-mile when he encountered a poor traveller of the roads playing a tin-whistle by the riverside. He was a small bearded man of sixty years or so with a merry twinkle in his eyes and a battered tweed hat pulled down about his ears. He reminded Oiney a little of old Terry of the Hills, and he stopped in his tracks.

'Good evenin', Father,' said the stranger.

'Oh, I'm not a priest. Yourself now, you seem to have the right Northern accent?'

'I'm from Donegal.'

'That's not far from Monaghan, is it?'

'Less than fifty miles I'd say as the crow flies. But who would want to be a crow except maybe to escape from prison bars!'

Oiney, being a Creevan lad, soon was sitting in the rushes beside the old Donegal traveller, talking about the town-lands and parishes of Monaghan and Donegal until the very stars of Heaven came out to listen. It was only the loud tolling of the monastery bell brought Oiney back to a different, sadder reality. 'Good Lord,' he exclaimed regretfully. 'I'll have to leave. But tell me, friend, where are you stayin' the night?'

The old fellow slapped a side-pocket triumphantly. 'I've me night-cap here. and it'll not be the first or the last time I've slept undher the canopy o' Heaven.'

'You'll do no such thing,' Oiney insisted, 'for I'll bring you into the Guest House where I'm in charge, well a kind of. But we'll need to tread cautiously, not to arouse Brother Placid.'

'Surely to God,' said the Donegal man, 'you couldn't arouse a man with a name like Placid?'

'You'd be surprised,' Oiney replied. 'In fact you'd have the quare oul' shock comin' to you.'

It was early on the following day that the reckoning was to come. Brother Placid had scarcely taken up his usual place on the broad stool in the souvenir shop when to his horror he saw this tramp stagger out of the Guest House and disappear into the nearby woods. He rushed up to Oiney, who had just failed to prevent his guest going out the main door.

87

'Who was that?' shouted Placid angrily.

Oiney kept a calm exterior. 'Ask and you shall receive,' he answered Placid. 'Knock and you shall enter! He was one of God's children. That's who he was.'

'God's children indeed,' snapped Placid. 'The Guest House is not for tramps and drunks. There's a green door in the monastery wall where they can beg for alms. You're far too soft-hearted, Brother Excelsis.'

Just then Oiney remembered an old tattered book at home called *The Lives of the Saints* written by a man called Butler. In a gloomy day of boredom he had read several chapters. 'Is it not true, Brother Placid, that Saint Martin, Bishop o' Tours, shared his cloak with a poor naked beggar he met on the road? Is it not a fact that Saint Damien, moved by their sufferings, went to live among the lepers? And here in Clunagh we can only have a remote green door. A day will surely dawn soon when we have a robot tuned to serve the poor and record their gratitude on tape.'

Placid was uncertain how to respond and suddenly Oiney, in his desperate urge to get away from not only Clunagh but O'Reilly as well, remembered something else. He rushed upstairs and quickly changed into the suit which had lain for long in the Lost Property room. It was not an exact fit but it would serve its purpose. He folded the robe over his arm and in that state appeared before the astonished Placid.

'Oh, think twice, Brother, think twice! Whatever shall I tell the good Boniface?'

'Tell him,' said Oiney, 'that Excelsis had a call from on High cancelling an' supersedin' all previous orders. Tell him I've been ordered by the Lord to broaden me mission, to go out into the great wide world an' convert the awful sinners that abound in it. In return for the suit, I'll donate me robe to the monastery. Goodbye, dear Brother Placid, goodbye an' pray for me!'

The Miracle Man

Oiney got lost in the woodlands around Clunagh and although it was his intention to catch up with the Donegal man and travel part of the road with him at the very least, this was not fated to be. It was by the sound of a passing train that he managed to guide himself onto a road he hoped might lead to Dublin. He only had the little money that the 'great man' O'Reilly had provided him with, but his new sense of freedom created a sweet buoyancy in his heart. Towards noon however his legs grew weary of the walking and added to this came a heavy downpour of rain which made him run for shelter in a hay-loft off the main road.

He lay down in the comfort of the hay, listening to the heavy raindrops lash the corrugated iron roof of the loft. He tried to make plans for his future. He would avoid the Killiney hotel owner like the plague. If there was anyone in Dublin who would help it would surely be Aileen, Shaun's friend, who worked at the Abbey Theatre. She might be disappointed at his desertion of monastic life, but then he had warned them all on the helicopter that he was quite certain he had no vocation. He would tell her how much delight it gave him to be her hero, but that he could not endure life with the silent Cistercians even for her sake. He would also explain to her the homicidal tendencies of a monk called Placid, and surely then she would understand his very good reasons for fleeing this dangerous monastery.

In a few months he could make his way back to Creevan, though he was still very much afraid of his granny. She had often threatened him as a boy that she would 'murdher' him; this time he was quite certain he had given her every good reason to fulfil that promise. He also remembered Jonjo in his high belfry above the village. The sexton would scarcely believe the strange adventures which had befallen him. After a while the rain ceased, and he resumed his journey again.

It was a strange world indeed to be born into, he thought, where a decent body had little or no say in the terrible things that can happen. If he had not gone to the Wake that fatal night, he might this very minute be flying kites with Jonjo on the Castle Hill. If he had refused to go to the prison Infirmary or on to its roof he might still be rotting in Armagh Jail. If he had not written those stupid notes for the daft psychiatrist, the greedy Governor would not be collecting his presents. Reality was so complex that it wearied poor Oiney's brain to even think about it, so he gave up fruitless speculation and merely sauntered aimlessly almost along the lovely green countryside.

It was early in the afternoon when, hungry and exhausted, he sat down on the slope of a ditch, staring idly at a sign-post on the other side of the road. One of the places named on it struck him as familiar. Roshinne – 2 miles. He recalled it as the home of the pious cousin of Brother Placid, the man called Pat McNulty. Hoping and praying that Pat was a wiser and calmer person than his relative, Oiney took the gamble and the side road into Roshinne. The gnawing hunger pains played an important role in his decision but neither was he averse to meeting a man of unusual piety in a world where, the good Church constantly reminded us, gross materialism was making gigantic strides, even in little Catholic Ireland.

In the picturesque old village he had little trouble in locating Pat's abode. Everyone knew Pat and had the kind word to say for him. So it was with confidence Oiney knocked on his door. A tall man with a kindly face and a perpetual smile in his warm, brown eyes came to the door. Although Pat had not yet the faintest idea who his visitor was, the boredom of this small village was such that it relished even thunder and lightning to relieve the monotony. 'I come from Clunagh monastery where Brother Placid spoke of you kindly,' said Oiney by way of introduction.

'Ah, come in! Come in! Dear old Duck's Belly! Tell me, does he still jump up an' down an' rattle his teeth?'

'Unfortunately yes, but otherwise he's quite normal. But he does hold you in the highest esteem for your great piety.'

Pat's cheeks wrinkled into a modest smile of pleasure. 'Of course, he's exaggeratin',' said he, genuflecting as he led Oiney past the red lamp burning under a huge picture of the Sacred Heart on the mantelpiece. 'The humdrum duties of ordinary life leave little time for real sanctity. Shall we say a decade of the rosary or maybe you'd prefer a cup o' tay first?'

'God forgive me but I'll go the tay. I've this terrible drouth. It will help clear me throat for the prayers.'

Though the tea was only what they call in Ireland shamrock tea (three leaves to a cup), Oiney found it hot, if not invigorating. The kindly Pat then extended a plate with a soda farl on it which Oiney grabbed rather greedily. When he had devoured the last crumbs, as though in penance and to please his host, he went on his knees under a picture of Saint Theresa and waited on Pat to join him.

'Oh no, it was her turn last Saturday,' said the holy man.

There were seven or eight pictures of saints and Oiney was perplexed. 'What about Saint Sebastian then?' he asked, pointing to a painting of the almost naked martyr pierced with several arrows.

'Oh, no, no, no,' said Pat, covering his eyes. 'I can scarcely endure the poor man's agony.'

'Saint Monica, the mother of the great Augustine then,' suggested Oiney.

'Not her either. Monica is for Tuesdays and this is Friday,' Pat replied. Then he shook his head. 'How could I ever forget? This is Friday, I'm sure. Then it's the turn of the little wooden crucifix on the wall beside the room door. Let's kneel there!'

Pat began the prayers and Oiney intoned the responses as they both knelt on a rough bit of carpet under the crucifix. Oiney noticed in a quick sidelong glance that Pat's face had such a pious, bland expression that only a halo was missing to bring it into perfect harmony with any saint's effigy on the walls.

Oiney's thoughts wandered as the prayers reached their conclusion. He was staring at the wooden cross when suddenly a flicker of movement on that holy object drew his startled attention. 'Pat, Pat?'

'What is it?'

'Pat, look! The crucifix is drippin' blood . . . Look!'

'Blood? Nonsense!' Pat arose to take a closer look. 'Begod, you're right. Your nose isn't bleedin' by any chance?'

Oiney felt one nostril and then the other and shook his head.

Pat looked up at the ceiling and stroked his chin thoughtfully. 'Perhaps it's a mouse the cat's killed in the attic?' Yet there was no stain on the whitewashed ceiling.

Oiney went over to the crucifix and had a closer look. 'Pat, look, it's the wounds that are bleedin', where the nails went.'

'Ah hold on, sir,' said Mr McNulty, 'one has to be most careful in scrutinisin' before comin' to conclusions. Let me see! Begod, you're right. Now, who would believe that? What day did you say it was? Ah, Friday. Isn't that a coincidence? Good Friday was the very day of the Cruci-fixion and the good woman in Germany had the stigmata on a Friday too. My God, but that's the shockin' coincidence!'

'What's stigmata, Mr McNulty?'

'Stigmata? Them's the jagged wounds on the palms o' her hands, miraculously induced, I'd say. But look at the crucifix yonder. Begod, that fella's goin' great steam, isn't he?'

Just then a knock sounded on the front door and Pat opened it to allow in a poor thin woman who had the season of Lent written permanently on her features.

'Have a seat, Annie Bryson,' said Pat, 'an' houl your tongue for a minit. I've a great secret to confide in you, a deeper an' more important secret, Annie, than the ears o' the ass o' King Laoghaire.'

'What is it, Pat, what is it?'

'You'll hardly believe it, Annie, but me friend an' I think that a miracle o' God has come to Roshinne.'

'Aye, Mrs Bryson,' said Oiney, trying to be helpful as usual. 'I'll vouch for it meself.'

Annie was almost overcome with emotion and dropped on her knees to the floor. 'Oh, glory be to Him in the highest. I always knew the good Lord above would never forget the good folk of Roshinne ... I always knew He'd favour us with a miraculous creation like He did Knock Shrine in Mayo, an' Brigid's Well in Faughert an' Saint Patrick's Purgatory in Lough Derg and God bless us an' save us, the preserved head o' Blessed Oliver Plunkett in Drogheda. Shure, God knows our wee land is brimmin' with miraculous shrines an' wells an' statues an' why should Roshinne be left behind ...'

'Now you're talkin', Annie, now you're talkin',' cried Pat with growing enthusiasm. 'Why should our poor forsaken wee village not have the coach-loads o' pilgrims to resthore our lost trade an' the faith o' poor sinners. Annie, get up on your feet an' take a good peep at the Man on the Cross, the Crucifix ... on the wall!'

Annie did so and almost fainted at what she saw. She drew back in fright and made the sign of the Cross. 'Holy mother o' God, Pat! Would you give me a chair before I drop stone dead! Oh, my God, I'll never get it out o' me mind ... the ... the Bleeding Crucifix o' Roshinne.'

'An' keep a quiet tongue in your head about it Annie,' cautioned Pat, winking at Oiney, 'for I don't want me good lino worn to shreds too soon.' He knew for certain this was the one effective way of getting Annie to spread the news.

Soon the whole village had heard about the great wonder of the bleeding crucifix, and, while the wise old men shook their heads, the McNulty house and the strange happenings there became the subject of many a stormy argument.

93

Memories were recalled of Pat's pious Aunt Mary, who had lived in that very house twenty years previously and who was widely regarded by everyone as a living saint, attending for twenty-five consecutive years every Mass, funeral, marriage, baptism, Benediction plus all the minor services ever held in Saint Claire's. As she had no family all her wordly possessions went to her nephew Pat, who was very fond of her. She had died of a brain tumour long before she had reached middle age. The village folk, therefore, had good cause to believe that poor Mary had some connection with the recent miracle. There was a saying in Roshinne that if anyone in the village ever earned the right to be in the arms of Jesus, it was Mary.

It was in Annie Bryson's house on the hill that many folk gathered to hear her account of the strange event. 'Oh, it wasn't just a dhrop,' she said, exaggerating somewhat, 'it came in torrents an' every bit as fresh as that day on Calvary hill two thousand years ago. An' if you ask me, I think the Lord is makin' up to Mary for the miracles denied her in her lifetime. I was with poor Mary the night o' her passin'. I mind it well, it was All Souls' Night, when the oul' graveyard beyont does be haunted. I heard Mary's last words. "I'll never forget Roshinne," she said with a wan smile on her lips, "I'll put in a good word for you all with the Almighty." An' them were her very last words.'

'Ah, shure, may God bless the dacint wee soul,' was the fervent prayer of all present.

'But I remember years before,' continued Annie, 'when Mary had her keen disappointments an' severe tests to her Faith. God only knows how she survived. I did some sewin' an' washin' for Mary as you all know. Well, one morning I seen this expression on her face of heavenly joy. She had said a prayer the night before that God would let her know the number of her days so that she could do as many works of mercy as she could before she died. And she imagined that God had given her a date. But the day passed and a year and another year but Mary was still walkin' the ways o' the world. I think her failed prayers nearly broke her heart. She never got over that. That's why I think that now she has God's ear in Heaven she's gettin' a bether response.

If millions an' millions o' people on earth are all seekin' favours at the same time, wouldn't God be hard put to give answers straightaway? I know I would.'

'My God Annie,' said Blind Packy, who was sitting by the stove. 'Haven't you the convolutin' tongue an' an imagination that stretches further than a voyage o' Brendan's! You should take up writin' them Kitty the Hare an' banshee stories for *Ireland's Own*. When the Lord gave poor Mary the date o' her demise maybe it was the Old Calendar He was goin' by. Someone should check up on that . . . He! He! Haw! Haw!'

'Someone should check up on you,' Annie retorted sharply. 'Blind is he, the disbelievin' oul' fox? Every time the Judge sits, Packy's undher his nose ferretin' out the secret sins o' the parish. Blind is it? Packy can hear the very grass grow an' he doesn't fool Annie Bryson one wee bit.'

There was a man in Roshinne however who took a very serious view of the Bleeding Crucifix, for he had the sorry experience of a similar 'miracle' in a remote corner of County Kerry. This was Sergeant Mannion of the local Civic Guards, or Garda as this body of the Law is known in the Gaelic. As a young constable he had allowed these rumours to spread until the Kerry village was swamped with hordes of frantic, eager pilgrims and scarcely any amenities to meet their daily needs. Pandemonium had been created and it had taken another miracle almost to disperse the crowds and get them back to the four corners of Ireland. Sergeant Mannion had learned his lesson.

This then was the stern officer who stormed into the McNulty home when he learned the news.

'What's this bloody nonsense all about Pat?'

'Nonsense? What nonsense?'

Like all good Irishmen, Pat had a sound distrust of law-enforcing agents.

'Come off it! This bleedin' crucifix all Roshinne's talkin' about!'

'Oh, the Crucifix! Oh that! I see what you mane. It was bleedin', but you can see it's stopped.'

This news had the Sergeant puzzled. 'But it *was* bleeding?'

'Aye, a while ago. Me friend from Clunagh Monastery saw it an' Annie Bryson saw it.'

'You'll be tellin' me next that Blind Packy saw it,' snapped the Sergeant with heavy sarcasm. 'You'll be tellin' me great lies like that.'

Then he turned to Oiney and the Creevan lad saw the Civic Guard with the hawk's eye looking at him wickedly from head to foot like he was measuring him for a coffin. 'Tell me then, where do you fit in?'

Oh here we go again, thought the frightened Oiney. It was bad enough getting involved with Shaun and the Cistercians and P.P. O'Reilly without getting mixed up in miracles. Was there no peace for a man in Ireland at all? 'Oh, it's quite all right, Sergeant, I just came here because I knew Placid in Clunagh. I saw the Crucifix bleed. I'll swear to that.'

'The only swearing you'll do is in Court, young man. I've been in Roshinne for ten years and there's been no trouble until you landed here. Can you explain that?'

Oiney stared at the ground and wished it would open up and swallow him. How could he tell the Civic Guard that trouble hounded him all around the four provinces of Ireland, that it was his constant companion and bed-fellow? Could he explain that? If he could, he could explain the mysteries of religion, including the miracle of Roshinne. The Sergeant was about to go for his notebook and pen when the door opened and Father Rice the Parish Priest arrived in a great flurry. He took the Sergeant aside but Oiney could hear him quite clear.

'Sergeant Mannion, we don't want any undue commotion or arrests. We want this to pether out slowly. Otherwise we'll be the laughin' stock of Ireland and the Outer Hebrides. No great damage has been done yet that can't be righted, but don't let's get excited! For we'd rue that day. It would do you no great favour either with the Chief o' the Garda in Dublin or the T.D.s an' Senators. Let me attend to this in me own way, for I think I know what's goin' on . . .'

'Very well Father, and I hope to God it's settled soon.' the Sergeant turned to Oiney and glowered menacingly. 'If you're not out of Roshinne prompt, I've got lodgings for you.'

'Who is this?' said the priest pointing at Oiney when the Civic Guard had left.

'Oh, just a young fella, Father, who knows me cousin Placid in Clunagh.'

'Well, I'd rather he wasn't here.'

Pat opened the room door. 'Go in there lad, till Father Rice an' I have a wee talk!'

The room door however proved small obstacle to Oiney's powerful curiosity. He listened eagerly, his ear against the keyhole.

'Now Pat,' he heard the priest say angrily, 'all this miracle nonsense'll have to stop. You can't be arousin' the emotions an' expectations of these poor people. I have only been in Roshinne a couple o' years, but I knew the last Parish Priest well. We spent three days' Retreat at Clunagh Guest House and he let me know Roshinne inside out. He told me, Pat, you were good with your hands, that you had mended his watch in no time and the church organ in a couple o' days. Oh, he told me all about you, Pat. The rollin' eyes in the picture o' Saint Francis, Pat . . . two drops o' mercury cunningly placed . . . and the fallin' petals o' Saint Theresa, the Little Flower . . . strung, Pat, with almost invisible thread . . . and the nails of the True Cross that probably came from a stable door an' manufactured in Birmingham. Pat, tell the truth! You just can't resist a miracle can you?'

Oiney's ears were glued even tighter to the door.

'You know how it is, Father. Shure it's only a bit of a joke, Father, to stir up life a bit in this god-forsaken oul' village. All the excitement it does create an' the wonder in folk's eyes. How the people must have cheered when Jesus walked on the waters! I'd have loved to have been there at yon great carry-on of the loaves an' fishes. I wonder was there any brown bread among the lot or a soda farl? Father, I'll tell you the truth which I never did to the oul' priest before you.

'I saw me poor Aunt Mary pray for miracles all her days an' what happened? She lost her father an' mother when she

97

was still young, an' she went into bad health herself. For all her chapel goin' an' prayin' night an' mornin' she had twelve years o' epilepsy an' screamin' headaches. Instead o' proper attention in a Dublin hospital, she was goin' to Knock Shrine an' Lourdes an' Faughert till eventually she died of the terrible tumour that was on her brain, an' the cause of half or maybe three-quarters of her visions. Miracles be damned Father! I rigged me own up. I bored tiny holes in the figure on the Cross, Father, and I ran these narrow, narrow tubes up by the back wall, an' comin out undher the floorboards. Undher the lino, Father, an' the bit o' carpet, I have a small rubber pump with this heavy red dye in it. Will I give you an exhibition, Father?' said Pat excitedly, proud of his workmanship. 'A few squeezes on the pump, Father, and you're made!'

'You'll do no such thing,' exclaimed the alarmed priest. 'And just you get your darn contraption dismantled till I exorcise this place of the evil spirits that occupy it includin' that fellow in the room there! I'm not sure at all he hadn't a hand in this. He's an innocent enough lookin' gawk, but them's the ones to look out for. Get that contraption down this minit, Pat McNulty, and that fellow out of Roshinne before we have brimstone an' gnashin' of teeth!'

'I believe, Father, I could manufacture them too, if I was hard put to it,' said Pat with a sigh.

Killiney

Oiney, glad to leave Roshinne and Pat McNulty behind him, reached Dublin that same night. The size of the city together with its many fine buildings amazed him. He walked about the streets in a daze passing Trinity College, Nassau and Kildare Streets up into that lovely little square, St Stephen's Green, where he admired the bust statue of the poet Mangan and shared some of his biscuits with the ducks at the side of a little pond. Then he retraced his steps down to O'Connell Street and along to the Parnell Monument beside the Rotunda and Findlater's Church. He was sad about the numbers of poor travelling women who sat on the pavement in Talbot Street begging alms from the public on its way to and from the northern railway. This was the sad contrast to all the fine buildings and shop windows packed with grandiose wares.

On the railway platform he talked to a porter who advised him to get lodgings at Iveagh House, which was not only clean but inexpensive. The warden of that hostel spoke to him next day in the foyer.

'I see you there hanging about, unsure o' whether to go this way or that. Well, take me advice, son, an' make your way to Saint Michin's! You haven't been to Dublin, son, unless you first shake hands with the Crusader in the vaults o' Saint Michin's. It brings luck, you see!'

So Oiney, in need of a bit of luck, set out for the old church in the very heart of Dublin.

Climbing down through a doorway, or access, low in the wall of the church which also housed the organ used in the first production of Handel's 'Messiah', he followed the small queue of sightseers past the coffins and the severed preserved heads of those patriot-barristers the Sheares brothers. The Crusader, with legs broken and crossed as was the ancient custom with Knights Templar, lay on a wooden, rectangular plinth. He was quite gaunt and leathery and, in Oiney's opinion, somewhat gruesome. Urged by the attendant to shake hands with the dead man for good luck, Oiney, with a shudder and somewhat unwillingly, did so. This eerie feeling crept over him and he thought he felt one of his fingers go numb.

He was glad to crawl through the opening in the vault wall into the clear sky again. Perhaps it was merely his imagination but he had this strange feeling that he was being followed. Then quite suddenly, before he could leave by the gateway, a cold, clammy hand brushed his cheek and came down on his shoulder with a steadfast grip. Oiney gave a start and almost dropped with fright. He turned slightly, as much as he could in that grip, and saw the grinning heavy-jowled chin of the man he was trying to avoid – P.P. O'Reilly.

'How . . . how did you know I was here?' gasped the bewildered and unhappy Oiney.

'Quite simple for a Dublin man,' said the smug hotelier. 'Every new visitor to the city presents himself sooner or later to the Crusader in Saint Michin's. It was only a matter of patience, an' Patrick Paul O'Reilly has plenty o' that. Though you are tryin' that patience sorely, me boy. I went down to Clunagh with clothes on Saturday, but you had broken our gentleman's agreement, hadn't you?'

Oiney squirmed with the pain as the grip tightened.

'You left Clunagh on Friday, didn't you? And got involved with that miracle-man in Roshinne. Sergeant Mannion, an old friend, gave me all the seedy particulars. You hitched a lift on a peat-lorry to Dublin that day. When are you goin' to settle down? Just tell me that!'

The hotel owner did not relax his hold on Oiney until they were both safely seated in the rear of a chauffeur-driven limousine. It was only later that Oiney discovered the reason why the driver kept glowering over his shoulder on every convenient occasion. Three hotel hands had already been sacked and the chauffeur was uncertain even about the security of his own position. A few driving lessons, a licence, and there was this bumpkin behind the steering wheel.

The Bloomsbury Hotel was the strangest place that Oiney ever saw and that included the jail and monastery. It faced towards the sea a little to the west of Killiney village. Though the view from it of the famous Martello Tower, where Stephen Daedalus the hero of *Ulysses* lived in the opening chapter of that book, was slight, P.P. O'Reilly did not hesitate to call it in his advertising brochure 'a fine, frontal view of the literary landmark'. 'The Bloomsbury' was a large Georgian house with extensions at the front and rear to make it a suitable and convenient residence for all the disciples and admirers of James Joyce who flocked to Dublin annually for Bloomsday, the celebration of the great day in June 1904 when Leopold Bloom, the Jew from Eccles Street, found immortality.

Given a small cubicle at the top of the hotel Oiney changed into the waiter's uniform that O'Reilly had pro-vided and presented himself in the foyer of the hotel to be introduced by his boss to a genteel, bright little lady who sat in an armchair by the reception desk.

'This is my wife Kathleen,' said the hotelier. 'Kathleen, this is the lad I was telling you about. A proper rapscallion. I had to corner him in St Michin's. He'll be our general factotum and what have you . . .'

'I hope,' said Kathleen almost under her breath, 'that he lasts longer than the others.' She gave Oiney a kindly glance of sympathy which immediately kindled a great liking in Oiney towards the lady. She was so different to the large overpowering O'Reilly that it puzzled the Creevan lad how the pair had ever come together. Kathleen arose from her seat and accompanied the new waiter around the foyer in a sort of conducted tour. She brought him to examine several brightly illuminated show-cases standing close to the walls of the carpeted hall.

Oiney stared bewildered at the first show-case, for inside the glass frontage was a black porter bottle stuck in a little heap of grey sand and dark green seaweed.

'What in the name o' Jesus is that bottle an' dirty sand doin' in there?' he exclaimed. 'Will I get a brush an' shovel to clean up the mess, Missus?'

'Over my dead body,' roared a voice behind him. 'That's precious Joyceana, you nitwit.'

'Oh, I'm sorry, Mr O'Reilly. Sure I've seen dozens of oul' bottles like that on the dung-hill in Creevan.'

'Not that bottle,' hissed O'Reilly. 'That bottle is the identical one that was "stogged to its waist in the cakey and dough" of the third chapter of *Ulysses!*'

'Cakey and dough,' said the bewildered Oiney.

'The stuff around it, you fool. The seaweed, sand and slime, scooped up from the "snot-green sea" at Ringsend.'

'Grr,' said Oiney moving to the next case. 'Clay tobacco pipes? You could buy them one time back home for a penny a piece. I used to blow bubbles with them.'

'Not them pipes you didn't,' sniggered the hotelier proudly. 'Them pipes were the proud possession of old Barnacle ... Nora Barnacle's father. Molly Bloom ... Joyce's wife, Nora.'

The trio moved on to another case, a small gold coin on a purple cushion.

'What would that be then?' asked Oiney.

'That's one of our rarer exhibits,' said O'Reilly. 'That's the very half-sovereign the poor, dull skivvy gave to that chancer Corley in the story "The Two Gallants" in *Dubliners*.'

'How do you know, Mr O'Reilly?' Oiney was about to ask when he was distracted by a loud guffaw in the company who were assembled near the bar in the corner.

If the objects in the glass cases caused him some amazement, the various self-proclaimed disciples of the famous Dublin author were even more astonishing. They were a motley crew of Irish, American and English high-browed rich poseurs. He had never been in such company before. They spoke the same language as him but they gave it such a high, nasal, whining twang that he could scarcely make out a word they said. And so many of their words were what was called in Creevan 'jaw-breakers'. These were enormous jaw-breakers like 'unphiloprogenitive onanist' and 'idiosyncratic psychosis'.

There were two Yale professors with strident voices arguing with an Oxford don about the precise time that Leopold Bloom broke wind on the 16th June 1904. Up and down the foyer strode the tall, lean aesthete Wingham Pratt, who had been hissed off the stage at a recent Edinburgh Festival show for masturbating publicly in *Nausicaa*, a stage version of one of the scenes in *Ulysses*. Critics, too, had hurt his sensitivity by saying that he was carrying his 'contemporary realism' a little too far.

Oiney left the main literary 'stream of consciousness' to proceed to a corner near the door where an artist with a yellow beard and a black beret was painting the scene outside of buildings and sky. Ah, thought Oiney, this is more in my line. I will understand this simple down-to-earth setting. He took a glance and then backed away in astonishment. It had nothing, absolutely nothing in common with the scene outside! Well, both did contain a sky; Oiney saw a calm, sunny day with a few clouds, but the artist painted a great mad whirling tornado full of teacups and vases while below lay a crudely sketched cromlech on which lay a tormented fish with one huge staring eye. Oiney scratched his puzzled head and asked a bystander, 'What in the name o' God is that?'

'Well, your guess is as good as mine.' The speaker had a broad Dublin accent which well suited his caustic manner. 'That's Philip Hadden Anker, the doyen of Greenwich Village who turns up in Ireland every Bloomsday, the day that equalled in the oul' country the Year of the Short Corn and the Year of the High Wind. Did his nibs O'Reilly not educate you in this?'

'Please, excuse me ignorance, sir,' said Oiney.

'Oh, don't let that worry you. We're all just learnin'. O'Reilly thinks he knows everythin', the big clown of a man. He can, I know, recite *Finnegans Wake* backwards, but honest to God, it sounds the same both ways to me ... I come here more to watch the antics o' these eejits, exhibitionists and careerists every man jack o' them ... Them two Yale professors and the Oxford don yonder have made a small fortune lecturin' on *Finnegans Wake*. Mind you Joyce is a unique artist and innovator, but these phoney idolators give me the pip. It's just self-adulation of the bourgeoisie ...'

'The what?' said Oiney.

'The middle classes. The butcher, the baker, the candlestick-maker and the vicar of Bray ... The dullest, deadliest class in history ...'

'Serve the wines,' ordered O'Reilly, drawing Oiney to the side and pointing to a wine tray on the bar counter. 'And stop talkin' to that cynic Costello. Some of these days I'll run him head-first off the premises, with the bitther oul' tongue o' his.'

In the process of serving the wines disaster struck. Oiney had served Wingham Pratt and had just moved back from the smell of his nauseating perfume when he collided with the easel and canvas and scattered the painting face-downward on the floor where grit and sand had been blown in. 'Oh, sorry, sorry,' exclaimed the shocked waiter, lifting the canvas and starting to clean away the grit.

O'Reilly descended on Oiney with his arm raised.

'You stupid, stupid clodhopper ...'

'Don't ... don't ... don't touch it!' exclaimed the painter in horror. 'Leave the grit! Leave the pebbles! It's superb! Supreme. The final effect I was searchin' for. A complete manifestation of haphazard existentialist creation. You have made my day. Let me shake your hand!'

'Oh it was nothin' nothin' at all,' said Oiney. He extended his hand for Philip Anker to shake, but when that exotic artist started to exclaim 'Let me embrace you,' Oiney, dreading the perfume as much as the embrace, fled to the bar and the protection of Mrs O'Reilly.

'Oiney,' said Kathleen, 'don't let it upset you! You don't belong to this set, and believe me, you're not the only one.' She gave a long sigh accompanied by a look of utter weariness. This surprised him, for he had long imagined that opulence and contentment went hand in hand.

'Listen, Oiney,' Kathleen said, as though by way of consolation. 'When they retire to the Martello this evening you and I can go on a literary tour o' Dublin in our own time. Now wouldn't you like that?'

Oiney had not the faintest idea of what a literary tour of Dublin meant, but if it took him away from the hotel and O'Reilly, even for an hour or two, he was all in favour of it.

O'Reilly and his entourage departed for the Martello. Kathleen returned in the chauffeur-driven limousine after seeing a friend off to Killiney railway station. With a dark scowl the chauffeur opened the door to let Oiney take a seat beside her.

'I've something very important to tell you after we jettison his nibs,' she whispered, nodding towards the driver. The car went speeding into the heart of Dublin as darkness descended.

'Pick me up at eleven at the Four Courts, Frank,' Kathleen ordered the driver, and Oiney and she stood on the curbstone until the car was out of sight.

There was a large public-house just off the main road. 'Let's go into "The Brazen Head" for a drink, Oiney. I feel done in.' She ordered up the drinks from a seat in the corner. 'This is a very, very old pub,' said Kathleen. 'Wolfe Tone used to have a refreshment here when he was studying at Trinity.'

'You mean to say,' exclaimed Oiney, his eyes lighting up, 'that Wolfe Tone, the great Irish hero, had a drink here one time? Wolfe Tone that's buried in Bodenstown ... In Bodenstown churchyard, there is a green grave ...'

'The same man. And if Tone was here, then the Emmets an' Miles Byrne, an' Russell an' Napper Tandy an' God knows who else was here.'

'An' we're here too, Mrs O'Reilly,' said Oiney with a strange pride. Outside, in the little yard that ran beside the open window, a folk-singer with a guitar was playing

'Patrick Sheehan', an old ballad of the last century. It was the first time since they met that Oiney had seen contentment on Kathleen's face.

'This is one of the few escapes I have, Oiney,' she confided in him. 'To come here of a Saturday maybe, or a Sunday, to hear some of the old songs of Ireland, none o' your arty stuff, or cowboy nonsense sung by some young chiseler from Inchicore. After this we'll go up to McDaid's off Grafton Street, where Peadar Kearney who wrote "The Soldier's Song" drank. I knew him well meself.'

They had a drink in McDaid's and then they went into a quiet wee pub near Talbot Street.

'This is where, they say, James Clarence Mangan wrote that powerful poem "Roll forth my song to the mighty river",' Kathleen whispered with awe. 'And they say too that Yeats and Synge used to come here for a gill. When it came near closing time W.B. Yeats used to stand up and recite, "I will arise and go now". So they say. Listen, Oiney!' Kathleen suddenly became very serious. 'I'm booking you into Moran's Hotel for a day or two here in Talbot Street. You can't possibly come back to Killiney after what I've seen. O'Reilly has built a real hate campaign against you Oiney, I saw it at the railway station.'

'What did you see Kathleen?'

'You know the platform notice where it used to read the word in big letters:

KILLINEY

Well, me husband P.P. has got them all worked up against you so much that they're all out to murdher you, Oiney. And in their burnin' anger they have added an "O" to the platform sign so that it now reads

KILLOINEY!

Oh, I've not the least doubt that if you go back, some of these dark nights they'll do you in. I'm all for bookin' you in Moran's quietly an' I'll see you safe out o' Dublin.'

Booked into Moran's Hotel Kathleen decided they would have a last drink before parting for the night. She chose a little, quiet public-house near Fairview Park; she was an old friend of the owner Tom . 'A shandy an' a sherry, Tom, a glass of sherry. Listen Oiney. This is where Brian Boru had a drink before the Battle of Clontarf in 1014 AD.'

Oiney looked around the sturdy walls in amazement. 'More than nine hundred years,' he gasped, 'and it's here still?'

'Oh it wasn't like this then,' explained Kathleen, 'it was probably a little shebeen o' clay and wattle made. Tom!'

'Yes, Kathleen my dear?'

'Didn't Brian Boru come in here for a pie an' a pint before the Battle o' Clontarf, Tom?'

'He did indeed Kathleen,' said Tom turning to Oiney. 'He sat on that very chair you're sittin' on this minit. There's not a man in the city o' Dublin can contradict that . . .'

An irate little man, red-faced and wearing a deerstalker hat, arose from his seat near the fireplace. 'I'm the boy who'll disprove your statement, for it's a downright libel on the oul' Catholic heroes of Ireland. How could Brian Boru ate a pie when the battle took place on a Friday, a Good Friday at that, an' him with no dispensation from the Pope to ate meat?'

'Sit down Boylan,' shouted Tom, 'or I'll put you out again!'

'An' sure, maybe it was an apple-pie,' Kathleen suggested helpfully. 'But irrespective o' the pie, them's Brian's swords an' shield on the wall. Isn't that so Tom?'

'I thought so meself Kathleen, until I turned the shield round an' found "Made in Hong Kong" on the back. The swords maybe but . . .'

'Oiney?'

'What is it Kathleen?'

'I like you Oiney, an' I want no harm to come to you. That P.P. O'Reilly's a brute. I don't know why I ever married him . . .'

'Why did you Kathleen? You're two different kinds o' peole entirely.'

She sat in silence for a moment or two, trying to

recollect her memories. 'He was different when I met him, Oiney. He professed to be a rebel like meself. He was a friend o' Michael Collins long before the Treaty . . . he was a member of the R.I.C. – the Royal Irish Constabulary – that was then the British Police Force in Ireland. O'Reilly was a sergeant attached to Dublin Castle. He brought Collins news of every move o' the enemy. I was left in the back streets o' Dublin with a son of another man. I had to fend for meself an' the boy, but he grew up to be a good lad, if a bit wild at times.

'My son knew I was goin' to marry O'Reilly but he only saw him as a policeman, a British one at that. The work was too important to Irish Freedom to risk it seepin' out. Even Collins forbade it. I didn't know that Collins would've signed that damned Treaty . . . James Connolly would not have signed it . . . But he signed it an' got himself executed at Beal Nam Blath. I didn't know, Oiney, that O'Reilly would rise to be a Superintendent of the Irish Civic Guards undher that horrible blue-shirt General O'Duffy . . . I didn't know these things at the time. Honest to God I didn't. Never even guessed . . .'

Kathleen sat back on the chair, almost exhausted, while Tom laid another drink in front of her.

'It's alright Kathleen, it's on me.'

'I may as well finish me story Oiney. Once the twenty-six counties of Ireland were created an' that ugly Border established, Cosgrove, O'Duffy, Blythe, Mulcahy, the lot o' them didn't care a damn. The church neither. Irish Freedom was jettisoned by that crew. They carved out careers for themselves in politics, businesses and the Army. Before O'Reilly retired on his big pension he didn't give a frig about James Joyce or anyone else in literature or art. I heard him with me own two ears back in the twenties swear he would willingly shoot Joyce for corruption of literature and using filthy words. But now they've made a business out of Joyce an' poor Paddy Kavanagh up north . . . But I'll never see me son Shaun again, for he walked out of the house the day I said I was marryin' the R.I.C. man O'Reilly. I'll never see Shaun, an' me other son's stuck in that snooty college in Tipperary . . .'

Oiney could scarcely believe what he had just heard. He took Kathleen's hand in his own and held it gently. 'Kathleen, did O'Reilly not tell you that I come from Creevan?'

Kathleen wore a startled expression. 'Creevan? You don't!'

'I do Kathleen, an' what's more I've met your son Shaun.'

'Met Shaun?' she stared straight ahead of her as though she could not absorb this almost incredible news.

'Yes Kathleen, and I can find him for you. I know who will bring him to you. Aileen at The Abbey. She's great, Kathleen, she'll bring you and Shaun together.'

Mrs O'Reilly was naturally in tears of joy at this heartening news. Her spirit soared with delight as she listened keenly to Oiney narrating his tale of the Wake and the mad Customs Officer and all the strange, strange folk that walk the green fields of Erin. She called for a taxi and left Oiney off at Moran's Hotel. He gave her a little farewell kiss and promised he would go in search of Aileen that very next day.

Barrow Boy

During his stay in Clunagh Monastery and guest house he had thought about Aileen, remembering their first meeting that cold night on the roof of Armagh Jail. His heart gave a great surge of delight as he saw her now approaching on the roadside close to the kerb. Her pretty face was slightly flushed as she pushed a kind of trolley-barrow towards the stagedoor of The Abbey Theatre. She was wearing a deep orange-coloured headsquare but the same dark green suit as before. She did not recognise Oiney at first but when she did she drew the barrow to a halt. She stared at him in amazement.

'Oiney,' she exclaimed, 'where's your robe? I just don't believe it! Let me feel you! Are you real? I just don't believe it.'

'You an' Shaun an' Sheamus had no right whatever in incarceratin' me in that monastery,' said Oiney quite angrily, 'an' if more important matters hadn't arisen, I don't think I would ever speak to you again.' He then went on to describe how he had met Kathleen, Shaun's sad mother, who was married to that dreadful creature O'Reilly, and how she realised the terrible mistake she had made.

'My heart breaks,' Aileen replied with sadness in her eyes, 'for the unfortunate women of Ireland. Shackled in slavery. And I'll bet you she doesn't even believe in the Pill, does she?'

'Does she what?' asked the puzzled Oiney.

'Believe in the Pill? Don't tell me you don't know what the Pill is?' Poor Aileen looked so exasperated that Oiney wished they had taught him more than religion at that school on the hill.

'Never mind Oiney, about the Pill meantime! We must do something about Kathleen right away. Shaun's presently in Belfast. But wait! If I could find one of the women to take my place with the barrow tomorrow, I could go up north then and fetch Shaun down. I'm working at the theatre this evening. Tell you what Oiney,' she continued, 'I'm takin' this yoke here up to my place on the North Circular Road and if you wait I'll be back within the hour.'

It was only after she left him that Oiney wondered why she was pushing a barrow along the streets of Dublin. He had not seen much on the barrow, only a few bundles of pamphlets on the shelves with some cardboard boxes, while three or four queer-looking balloons tied to the shafts floated over the lot.

It was early afternoon when they met again and Aileen suggested that they take the bus out to the Dublin Hills beyond the Hell Fire Club. On the journey Oiney learned a great deal about his youthful companion. She had been born and bred on the Antrim Road, Belfast, under the shadow of the famous Cave Hill mountain where the brave United Irishmen had planned the 1798 Rising. Her father, a Catholic shipyard worker, had been murdered in an Orange pogrom in the Musgrave Channel, part of the Harland and Wolff complex. Struggling for his life in the water where he had dived to save himself, they had hit him on the head with iron bolts. Although a Catholic herself, she regarded her Church as wrong in some respects about politics and women's free rights in Ireland. In this respect she regarded it as mediaeval. She had no bias against Protestants, her sister, Jenny in fact had married one of that faith, but Orangism she detested, regarding it the same kind of reactionary disease as the Ku Klux Klan and Fascism.

Oiney and Aileen sat together in the moss and bracken of the hills above Dublin Bay. It was a lovely summer's day when Ireland looked her grandest. He would retain a nostalgic memory of this day forever.

'I tried to find someone,' said Aileen 'to do my rounds with the barrow tomorrow, but up to date I've had no luck. No one seems to be free.'

'I'll watch it for you then,' Oiney volunteered, only too eager to get Shaun down from Belfast.

'If you do that'll be fine. I'll show you the streets. The Durex packets cost two shillings; the pamphlets, well I'll explain about them later.'

'The Durex,' said Oiney with a puzzled look. 'What sort of a thing is them?'

'The Durex . . . the contraceptives!'

'The contrawhat?'

'The contraceptives. Oh don't tell me you do't know about them at your age!'

'Oh yes of course,' said Oiney quickly, not wanting to appear ignorant in Aileen's lovely eyes. 'Yes, indeed. The contraceptions!'

'You see Oiney, we're pro-abortionists. You understand?'

Oiney nodded eagerly. If Aileen was a pro-abortionist that was good enough for him.

'The pamphlets on the barrow are to be handed out free of charge. We don't want any more of those backstreet abortions, do we?'

'Indeed an' we don't,' exclaimed Oiney, wondering what they were. 'We don't want any more backstreet abortives, not if you say so Aileen. An' how much do the balloons cost?'

She gave him a sharp inquisitive look. 'Now Oiney, stop your fooling. Peter Flynn blew up a couple of Durex for advertising and a bit of a laugh.'

Her hazel-brown eyes had a bright sparkle, and Oiney felt a great longing to kiss those rosy lips. 'Aileen, I love you.'

'I bet you tell that to all the girls in Creevan.'

'There's ne'er a girl in all Creevan or Carrick like Aileen,' he said quietly, and meaning every word of it.

The next morning, before she left for Belfast, he collected the barrow from Aileen. She told him to be careful and not to make himself the target of any fool's abuse. Oiney assured her that he would be on his best look-out, meaning that he would not let any thief steal his wares. For this reason when he entered into the old backstreets of the Liberties in Dublin he parked his barrow on the roadside between a Catholic church and a convent. It gave him such a warm feeling of security to be near such havens of sanctity. Then he began to declare his wares.

'Dulux an' contraceptions,' he shouted. 'We don't want backstreet abortives, do we? Dulux an' contraceptions, all for next to nothin'!'

A tall lean man with his hat at a jaunty tilt sidled over to him. 'Could I buy one o' your balloons,' he said, winking at Oiney.

'No sir, definitely not. Them balloons are not for sale.'

'Stop your nonsense,' said the customer, offering Oiney two shillings, 'an' give me one of your French Letters!'

'French Letters, French Letters,' said the puzzled Oiney. 'I am afraid, sir, you've come to the wrong shop. There's a bookshop in Nassau Street, or maybe you could ask for them in your local library.'

'Give me a Durex,' said the man irritably. 'You . . . you . . . you coillte . . .'

'Oh a Dulux! Certainly, sir. An' you can call me all the names you like, for I'm used to them.'

His trade at the barrow was not too bad at all, but some folk passed him by with an angry glare or turned their holy heads away. Oiney never in his life dreamt there were so many surly people in Ireland; they were not like the Creevan folk at all. Then he saw the nuns gathering in their black robes at the convent door shaking their fists at him, and in a short while the Parish Priest came out to the chapel door and began to splash quite a sprinkling of holy water in his direction. He was completely amazed by the strange antics all around him.

Just then a little pot-bellied man with a red nose, very poorly dressed, brushed past the barrow and tried to overturn it. When he failed he began to shout at the top of his voice, his cheeks and neck reddening to match the colour of his nose. 'We want none of your filth in holy Catholic Ireland. Christ didn't die on the Cross at Calvary for you vermin.'

For the life of him Oiney could see no connection between his barrow and the Crucifixion, although he was soon destined to resolve that enigma. He was drawing the sad conclusion that quite a number of Dublin folk were utterly irrational when suddenly, and as though to verify it, he heard a loud shout, and a great mob descended on him. Led by the Parish Priest and the nuns, a larger crowd than had turned out for the Fenian Rising of 1865 descended on him. From the rear of the mob the little pot-bellied hero was shouting 'Let me at him! Throw the dirty sod in the river! Let me at him!'

And no doubt they would have done just that had Oiney not immediately grasped both shafts and pulled the barrow after him. He would not dream of returning to Aileen without a barrow. The angry mob still came in hot pursuit. An astonished Civic Guard at a crossroads made the way clear for them and then joined in the melée. Oiney puffed and panted up hill and down until he was utterly exhausted. He could go no further. He said a powerful last Act of Contrition that would surely help his invisible soul meet other invisible souls in an invisible world called Heaven: he finished it off with a wee prayer that his granny would forgive him for not bringing home the brown jug from Doyle's Wake. The rest was darkness. He collapsed under the barrow and the crowd, unaware of his presence even as they followed their leaders, pressed him deeper and deeper into the hot tarmac until he was almost invisible.

When he came to several hours later he thought for a moment or two that he was in Purgatory. He was lying on his back staring at a whitewashed ceiling. His pain-racked body was dressed in a brown habit not unlike a monk's robe. His arms were folded across his chest and his fingers clasped the crucifix of a pair of rosary beads. A holy candle burned in a dirty saucer at his feet. The only really incongruous object in this scene of piety was a bottle of cheap wine, half empty, which sparkled in the candlelight. Then Oiney heard a gruff voice ascend in the shadows. 'Give us another swig o' that, Barney!'

A weathered sinewy hand came out of the darkness, lifted the bottle and drew it quietly into the shadows.

Oiney lay there still and silent, his head in a great turmoil. The only man he had ever seen dressed like this was at the Wake in Doyle's parlour. The Creevan lad was tongue-tied with astonishment and horror. Surely someone was making a terrible mistake, thinking that his soul had parted from his bruised body? And then he heard another voice that was somehow vaguely familiar.

'This young fella,' said the voice, 'has led the quare oul' life. The last time I met him he was nothin' less than a monk in charge of a Guest House in a monastery in Tipperary.'

'A monk begod,' exclaimed the other with awe in his voice. 'A long journey that, to the mud o' Dublin. Still, he's some poor woman's son, God help her.'

'Oh, he was decent enough to me,' said Barney. 'That's why I took special pity on the poor fella an' him dead . . .'

Oiney could scarcely believe his ears. It was none other than the Donegal travelling man. Even if he had wanted to the Creevan lad would have found it very difficult to jump up, no matter his delight to be alive. Instead he lay there still and silent and even beginning to enjoy his Wake. The conversation, however, as it continued, became less complimentary.

'I think,' said Barney, 'this fella had somethin' wrong with his brain-box.'

'How is that, Barney?'

'Well, for one thing, he puts me between clane white sheets an' me with no bath for weeks. He probably got his books from Clunagh, 'cause they're awful fussy about good honest dirt down there. An' next thing, the daft fella's sellin' French Letters in the backstreets o' Dublin. Did you ever hear of a Cistercian monk sellin' Durex?'

The two old hoboes were doubled over with laughter and sharing the bottle between them. They were even daring to tackle Church Law. 'What makes the Catholic Higher Archy down on abortion so much Barney?'

'Hierarchy, you mane?'

'Aye, that's what I said. Higher Archy. The top brass!'

'The Pope, the Bishops, the lot I suppose,' said Barney, taking a last swig at the bottle, 'I suppose it's all a question of population. The more abortions the less Catholics. There was a woman not long ago in the County Fermanagh died, leaving twenty-two children, one for every year of her married life. What a poor, terrible existence! I don't think that God bothers His head one wee bit about abortions. D'you know, Danny, that God kills off about a hundred and ninety-nine million spermajigs an' just lets one reach the stage o' conception . . . Did you know that Danny?'

'Bejasus I didn't. An' isn't it the shockin' waste? Shure, if He was God couldn't he have just created one or two in the first instance an' not waste His valuable energy an' material?'

'If you ask me Barney, God would be a lot more concerned with the numbers of wee children murdhered in their millions in war and unnecesary famine. There's no dispute there about whether they're six or eight weeks in the womb. They're six and eight years old when their lives are aborted. That's the rale mass murdher, Danny. That's what your Church should be declaiming, an' lave the poor mothers alone!'

'An' yet Barney, you say this fella was a bit quare to risk his neck?'

Oiney squirmed uncomfortably.

'Bejasus Barney,' said Danny startled, 'Did you see that?'

'Did I see what?'

'The corpse twitched, Barney, the corpse twitched. I seen it with me own two eyes. If you'd ask my opinion, I'd say this corpse is only half-dead! There it goes again!'

'Half-dead me arse,' said Barney. 'This corpse is as dead as the Dail in Dublin. It's just the last twangin' o' the nerve cells ere rigor mortis sets in. Though there was the instance of a man up the street, Tim Finnegan by name, who got up from his own wake, drank all the porter, lit a pipe an' then lay down again an' died dacintly.'

'Rigor mortis be damned,' cried Danny, taking to his heels hotly pursued by Barney, as the corpse sat up.

'Come back! Come back!' pleaded Oiney. 'I want to thank you both for rescuing me. That's better. Barney, Barney, there was never a man I was so glad to see. But what did you do with me clothes!'

'Tell him, Danny,' said Barney sadly.

Danny searched his pockets and produced a crumpled pawn ticket. 'We got the woman next door to clane an' iron your waiter's suit an' then we had to pawn it, hadn't we, for the shroud an' the candle . . .'

'An' the wine,' said Oiney.

'Shure, when we dug you out of that tarmac you were as flat as a pancake.'

'Well,' said Oiney, 'I'll need to get me clothes back.'

The two men, shrugging their shoulders and obviously unable to raise any money to redeem the pledged suit, backed quietly out of the room, leaving the unfortunate Oiney to resolve his problem as best he could. He would not dare send a message to Aileen, for apart from losing her barrow, she would howl with laughter if she saw him dressed like this. And Kathleen, for all her personal sadness, might just do the same.

He had now no option but to walk boldly through the streets of Dublin. It was midday and the city was at its busiest, which perhaps was as well, for with the dense crowds on the pavements very few pedestrians got a full-length view of him. Some children however did, and immediately burst out giggling thinking he was going to a fancy dress party. Several old women saluted him, mistaking him for a Franciscan priest. Most folk merely passed a sidelong glance and took him for some foreign ambassador.

The pawnbroker's hair stood on end when Oiney, the pallor of his face contrasting with the brown shroud, handed his pawn ticket over the counter. The frightened man made the sign of the Cross and said his Jesus Mary and Joseph. Some of his customers undoubtedly made very long journeys to redeem their pledges but this, surely, was the first ever to return from the other side.

The sad tone in Oiney's voice moved even the pawn-broker. Besides, he worried about the apparition being bad for his business. And so Oiney, restored to life and having changed into his suit in the cubicle, walked joyfully into the glorious sunlight of Dublin city.

The Trick Cyclist

As things turned out it was a rather crestfallen Oiney who had eventually to report the loss of the barrow to that ardent activist Aileen. The fact that she was so busy striving to unite Kathleen and Shaun might serve to distract her a little and soften the blow. Yet Oiney felt that he must somehow find a job and raise the funds for another barrow.

A note from Kathleen left in Moran's hotel requested his presence at six o'clock that evening under the arched entrance to Trinity College at the foot of Grafton Street. Although Oiney had suffered many alarming experiences and was becoming slightly inured to them, the thought of meeting Shaun, Kathleen and Aileen at the one time set his nerves jangling. Near six o'clock he walked over O'Connell Bridge on his way towards the historic venue. Swift, Tone, Emmet, Goldsmith, Davis, Sheridan and many other prominent people had passed under this proud archway.

The others were awaiting his arrival. There were tears of joy in Kathleen's eyes and even Shaun seemed to have lost some of his aggressiveness as, arms linked, the four friends began their walk of the cobbled quadrangle. First there was some eventful news to narrate. Kathleen told how in a fit of rage at the idea of Shaun's return P.P. O'Reilly had rushed out of the Bloomsbury Hotel, swearing loudly that Oiney was the source of all his bad luck and that misfortune had trudged him since ever he had set eyes on that pious fraud in Clunagh Guest House. He vowed as well that Oiney's neck would be more twisted than a corkscrew if ever he should lay hands on him.

'An' where did you leave me barra?' Aileen asked anxiously. Oiney then stammered out the sad tale of his misadventure.

'My God,' exclaimed Kathleen, 'd'you mean to say you hadn't a cup o' tay in all that time or since?'

'Divil the cup or morsel has passed me lips,' said Oiney.

'Well, we'll soon make up for that in Grogan's Bar,' Kathleen assured the company, 'for we've real cause to celebrate at me meetin' me son Shaun again.'

In the privacy of Grogan's lounge Aileen also had a word of comfort for Oiney. 'Don't worry about the barra, Oiney, just don't! There's a lot a spare wood lyin' around the theatre backstage an' we'll knock somethin' together. I'm not goin' to let the holy brigade put me off me mission. I'm not indeed.'

But Shaun was more annoyed: 'I don't know what it is Oiney, but you have the unfortunate habit of muckin' things up. If you had stayed in the monastery where you were put none of this would have ever happened.'

'And no one would have ever brought us together,' said Kathleen, 'would they? Leave the poor fella alone! Remember he's just a young country-boy from the backwoods o' Creevan, as innocent as meself one day. But Oiney, keep clear of the south o' Dublin. O'Reilly an' me are partin', an' he's vowed revenge. The Bloomsbury's in my name an' we're turnin' it into a hostel where the wives of political prisoners can meet, and girls who have gone through the despicable ordeal of strip-searching. There'll be a room downstairs where qualified staff under the aegis of Aileen an' her group can give sound advice on abortion. We're callin' it The Sanctuary. Another thing. I'm takin' me son Luke out o' that snooty-nosed college in Tipperary. He can come home and study for Trinity or U.C.D. or whatever he likes, in one of the day-schools.'

Aileen had a suggestion too for Oiney: 'You could do a lot worse,' she said, 'than get yourself any wee job in the north side o' the city. You could learn a bit about city life, for God knows, some country places in Ireland are still a hundred years behind the times. You could go into cheaper lodgings. I saw some jobs advertised only this mornin' in a shop window at the corner of Gardener Street.'

Thus it was that Oiney came to be interviewed by the Manager of Fairview Toy Factory, not far from the pub in Clontarf where Kathleen and him had been recently. The bald and very important looking manager was not entirely convinced that this country chap had all the necessary qualifications for this important job. But he was willing to give him a fair trial.

'This task,' he assured him, 'will require your maximum concentration. It's what we call a precision job. A wrong move to the left or the right would be a calamity. You will require a training period, perhaps, at a reduced salary, of course.'

Oiney was on edge with excitement at the prospect of his first real job. He told Aileen the great news.

'What exactly do you do?' she asked.

'I don't know what it is, but it sounds real important. Precision is the key word. I just can't wait. Isn't it exciting?'

The following day the manager showed him around the toy factory and then into an annexe where seven girls were assembling hobby-horses on a conveyor-belt system. His guide brought him to the end of the belt where there was a large pile of batches of black hair. The manager without any ado lifted a single batch, dipped one end of it in a large pot of hot glue and then stuck it with unerring accuracy plumb on to the bald hindquarters of a recently painted hobby-horse. Another and then another. 'You'll understand now what I meant yesterday by precision,' he said.

The amazed Oiney looked at him hard to see if he was serious, but there was not even the hint of a smile on that grim countenance.

'D'you think you can cope?' he asked Oiney.

How could he possibly fail, Oiney wondered, unless by chance he lost his eyesight or the use of his hands. He merely replied however that he would try to be accurate and, giving the manager an assuring exhibition of his ability in sticking tails to the hobby-horses' behinds, he was left to continue on his own this most edifying and noble task.

Oiney for the life of him could not imagine a more monotonous and soul-destroying job. Admittedly the horses were painted in a variety of colours – black, brown, white, grey and piebald, but the tails were uniformly, without exception, jet black, all of equal girth and each exactly eighteen inches long. Occasionally as the day dragged on one or other of the girls would smile over at him in sympathy. He, however, for a good part of the time kept watching the clock for the happy hour of his release, and when eventually it came, no one could run faster to the gates. He had not enough humour in him to tell Aileen or anyone else the exact nature of his job. They might, on being told, tell him of the great happiness he was giving children, but then they would turn their faces away to hide their laughter.

On the way home past the wide curve of the open road he often stood to watch the amazing performances of passing cyclists who, coming from their various places of work also, had to pass a Catholic church at this rather dangerous corner. The dexterity of these cyclists really astonished him and it became almost a ballet of extreme beauty as they raised their right hands from their bicycles and made the sign of the Cross. It all recalled to his memory that fantastic day long ago in Creevan when the Circuit Judge had entertained the village on the icy brae. Oiney vowed that he would keep sticking tails until he had at least enough money to buy a bicycle.

Eventually that happy day dawned. Before riding it to work, however, Oiney practised each morning and evening in a quiet corner of Fairview Park. When he had learned to ride he still had the task of holding the handlebars steady with one hand while he blessed himself with the other. The bike wobbled unsteadily on his first few attempts but after a time he mastered the feat and was at long last fit to take his worthy place on the thronged roadway.

He felt a great pride and delight as he joined his fellow cyclists on the sweeping curve past the church. Then, in harmony with them, in a wonderful declaration of Faith, he raised his right hand from the handlebars: 'In the name of the Father, and of the Son, and of the Holy Ghost, Amen.' His face beamed in holy delight, and then . . .

He can never explain it to this day what tempted him to take his other hand off the handlebars to complete the perfect blessing. Perhaps it was an absolute trust in the Almighty to guide us through shadow and storm.

Whatever or whoever it was that tempted him, he was crazy enough to succumb. He sat back on his saddle, his face flushed with triumph at this superb miracle of Faith and looking around to see if any of the others were admiring his marvellous skill when the disaster struck. He did not notice the great puddle of water that soaked his tyres and caused him to take a long low slide at a rapidly diminishing angle which brought him into collision with more and more bicycles.

Dozens of bicycles and their riders piled up on the stretch of roadway and the pious ejaculations of a moment or two previous were now replaced by some of the loudest oaths he had ever heard in Christendom. Oiney lay at the very base of this squirming wriggling mass, but fearing for his life, he hauled himself and his bike to the far pavement and down a side road. Needless to say, after that dreadful experience, he never attempted even to raise his right hand from the handlebars but merely gave the church a courteous nod, knowing that if there was anyone up there, He (or She) would understand.

One Bishop has a Bash

Long, long ago when he was just a boy of ten years or so, Oiney's granny had him enlisted in the local Boy Scouts. One fine summer, Oiney remembered it well, the troop had gone on a camping expedition to Termanfeckan where there was stretches of fine sand. From this spot, it was no great journey by the seaside to march into Drogheda on the river Boyne, where in 1690 King James had lost the battle but won the race into Dublin.

The young Scouts were taken to see the preserved head of Oliver Plunkett (now canonised) in a side tabernacle at Drogheda cathedral. The shuddering memory of that visit remained vividly in Oiney's young mind for the simple reason that, like the Crusader whom he had recently seen in Saint Michin's, the head of Blessed Oliver did not look the least preserved. The face was awful grey-like, thought the boy as he stared at the glass door in the tabernacle. If God had really wished to preserve the saint's head, surely thought Oiney, could He not have done it decently and given him a nice, fresh, smiling face to show that he was happy above. That kind of display would be certain to convert everyone, except Orangemen of course.

Oiney had discussed his grave doubts with Jonjo the day after his return from camping. 'I'm sorry, Oiney,' said the sexton, after thinking the matter over. 'Now put yourself in his shoes. I don't think you would be in a happy smilin' mood, if your head was being chopped off be an English axe-man. Another thing. Maybe you saw him in a black mood — on one of his off-days. Maybe he was feeling a bit morose. Saints I suppose do have their ups and downs like the rest of us.'

Oiney thought this was a rather threadbare explanation, so now that he had his bike and a free Sunday, he decided to cycle up to Drogheda and have another glance at the tabernacle. He rode through Kerries and the other pleasant little villages by the north of Dublin and then cut in by the ancient plains of Meath to the large cathedral town. He left his bicycle behind the gate wall and made towards the side aisle where the tabernacle was situated. Something strode towards him out of the shadows and Oiney gave a sudden look of recognition: 'In God's name, Pat McNulty, what are you doin' in Drogheda!' exclaimed Oiney. The words were scarcely out of his mouth when he realised his mistake. The man was wearing a clerical collar.

'I'm Father Twomey,' said the priest. 'I'm sorry, I'm not you Mr McNulty. I'm the sacristan. Would you like to see Blessed Oliver?'

He was a nice, gentle-faced man and spoke so warmly about the saint that one felt that Oliver was alive and well. The priest led the way up the aisle to where the candles burned in a shining brass tray and lit up a small, veneered oak stall where a collection of slim pamphlets lay with the rather rhetorical title of 'Do Miracles Happen in Ireland?' Oiney was about to express the severe testing that his Faith was undergoing, when suddenly he had a glimpse of the tabernacle: the cheeks of the saint had a somewhat ruddy glow, and his entire appearance seemed so different from what Oiney had seen on his last visit. 'Father Twomey,' gasped Oiney, 'I just can't believe it. Oliver seems to grow younger an' better-lookin' with the years. Do you do him up?'

'Nonsense, young man,' said the priest. 'Miracles are divine manifestations. Surely you don't imagine . . .'

'Oh, it's nothin', Father. It's just I'm amazed to see him lookin' so fit an' well. A great change for the better.'

Oiney made a quiet retreat down the darkened aisle. He was about to leave the cathedral when he halted in his tracks. Above a confessional box at the rear of the aisle, he detected a slight movement. He stood for a moment gazing in wonder. There: it moved again. A large painting of Judas hanging himself in the garden was moving up and down.

My God, thought Oiney, this place is surely brimming with miracles! He was about to call Father Twomey's attention to this strange phenomenon when the priest disappeared into the sacristy.

He looked up again to see the picture come off the wall completely, and standing on top of the confessional was a tubby little man who shouted, 'Hey, you there! Give me a hand down with this! It's for cleanin' an' restoration!'

Being a kindly fellow, as we all know by this time, Oiney gave the industrious man a helping hand, and even put his shoulder to the picture to assist in carrying it down to a van which lay parked a little down from the main gates of the cathedral. It was only now that he was able to see the man's face clearly for the first time, and when he did so he was truly astonished. For this was the very man who had been roughly thrown into his cell in Armagh Jail the week before his escape! None other than Bobby Brown the Belfast Protestant! 'Well, of all the wondhers o' the small world,' said Oiney, shaking hands with Bobby warmly, so delighted was he to see him, 'an' what in God's name are you doin' in Drogheda, Bobby? Have you the good job at the resthorin'?'

'Well, to tell you the truth, I haven't restored anything yet. I've taken but not restored if you know what I mean. An' the job, like many another has its ups and down. I was up when you seen me, up on top o' the confession box . . .'

'You mean to say you . . . you are stealin' this holy picture an' I'm helpin' you . . . I'm helpin' you?'

Bobby nodded his head. 'I'm sorry, Oiney, but what you say is only too true. But I did take your advice . . . the advice you gave me when we first met. I haven't touched an offering-box in a church or chapel ever since. I only do cathedrals now, an' believe me, Oiney, yours was sound advice. There's far better pickings.'

Oiney felt a wave of disgust flow over him. 'Bobby Brown, we're puttin' that picture back. I've made up me mind, an' I don't want to have to tell that sin in confession . . . and I'm not lettin' you steal church property. I'm definitely not goin' to be part or parcel of this.'

'Oh, just this once, Oiney,' pleaded the icon-stealer. 'It's only for Jenny an' the four children. You wouldn't have

126

them starve, Oiney. You wouldn't have them cryin' out for fish suppers last thing at night, would you? All for one oul' paintin'? Remember I helped you out of jail? Just this once, Oiney.'

'Well, just this once,' said Oiney softening, thinking that one picture would be no great loss to a church that has riches beyond measure and countless art treasures. Oiney then said farewell, but when he returned to where he had left his bicycle it was gone. Frantic, he searched rapidly around the buttresses of the cathedral, but there was no sign of it at all. He then hurried back to the van and told Bobby the sad news.

'God above,' said the Belfast man. 'Some folk have no piety about them at all. They'd even steal from sanctified ground. Tell you what, Oiney. We'll run this painting into a store I have in Dundalk, and then I'll give you a lift back to Dublin.'

On their way into the grand old town of Dundalk, Oiney thrust his concern about his lost bicycle out of mind for the time being, and began a conversation with the driver. 'Tell me, Bobby, how did you know a helicopter was comin' to lift me off the Infirmary roof?'

'Ah, that'd be tellin' you the secrets o' the game, Oiney. But I'll give a wee clue. Does the letter "A" ring a bell?'

'Aileen?'

'Aye. I'm married to her sister Jenny, so there's the tie-up for you. She's a great girl, Aileen, an' not an ounce of bigotry in her. I'm a Protestant an' honest to God she couldn't care less, whether I was a Hindoo or a Hottentot.'

Oiney, tired from his cycling and his work in the toy factory, fell asleep, but not for long. On the edge of Dundalk six rather vicious Civic Guards surrounded the van, and finding the stolen painting, arrested the icon-stealer and Oiney. Soon they were lodged in the local prison and charged with pilfering Judas Iscariot and desecrating sacred ground.

'No wonder Christ wept in the garden,' shouted Bobby kicking the cell door and demanding a lawyer. He gave Oiney the few pounds he had on him and asked him as a favour to approach the local Bishop on his behalf and plead for clemency. To be fair to Robert Brown, he exonerated Oiney completely and took all the blame on his own shoulders, saying that he had merely given his co-accused a hitch on the road to Dundalk.

On a bright summer's day, the Bishop of Meath sat in his study basking in the delight of the lovely countryside. He was a stout, ruddy, jovial man with three or four chins all of which rippled with laughter, especially at good clean harmless jokes of religious origin, jokes, he believed, that even God Himself would enjoy. As he sat back in his plush armchair, he often thought to himself: why should atheists and the like have all the fun? He felt he had earned his comfortable bishopric after many years of service in the Missions abroad. The study was large and luxurious with a great sideboard displaying ivy and jade ornaments, trophies and gifts acquired during his more hectic years in Africa, India and China. At the far end of the study there was a wide, magnificent bay window leading on to a verandah overlooking a well-kept lawn which was occasionally used as a tennis court. His grounds were surrounded by rhododendron bushes and presently the soft breeze bore their pleasant perfume through the open window.

He was sitting back in his beloved armchair reading anecdotes of the great Dean Swift. One of them in particular had his several chins sagging and wagging. It was the letter the Dean had written to his superiors in London who, after exiling the great man to the fairly obscure post of the deanery in Dublin and giving in his stead high bishoprics to inferior and sometimes worthless clergymen, had the effrontery to enquire from Swift if the recently appointed new bishops had arrived in Dublin. Would the Dean please inform them? The great man was furious as he reached for his quill: Gentlemen, wrote Swift, it seems as if the three bishops who were appointed in London were proceeding to Hollyhead, when they were waylaid by three highwaymen in the woods in Wales who stripped them of their clothes and worldly possessions, and disguised as bishops, these three gentlemen have landed in Ireland at Kingston.

As the Bishop of Meath rocked with laughter, his faithful servant Christine entered the study. 'Sorry, my lord, but your visitor has arrived.'

'What visitor is that, Christine?'

The servant was accustomed to his absent-mindedness. 'The lad who wrote you the letter, a Mr Oiney Hoy.'

'Oh, oh yes. The one who penned that strange epistle, utterly outside my comprehension. Do show him in!'

Oiney, gaping at the magnificent splendour of this heavenly representative, was ushered into the study. 'Sit down, young man! And tell me now, what can I do for you?'

The nervous Oiney sat down in front of the Bishop, and poured out his heart in a fervent plea for his imprisoned friend. He told the good Bishop the man's sad story, how he had lost his parents when he was but of a tender age, how he had been slightly corrupted by a well-meaning but weak clergyman, the lone years he had spent in Homes and Borstals, how he had lost his best job through his generosity to poor Irish emigrants on the ship, how his broadmindedness had allowed him to marry a Catholic and how he had four equally sad little children. Oiney went on to narrate a few of Bobby Brown's minor faults, how he was given to dipping in church collection-boxes, which, of course, was wrong as these boxes were for the poor. Yet wasn't it only a time difference if one looked at it sensibly? Wasn't Bobby himself poor and only taking in advance what was his by right? His sin, therefore, was surely only of impatience. His biggest mistake, Your Worship would agree, was that of stealing the oil painting out of Drogheda Cathedral. But surely the great wealthy Church could easily afford one painting if the value of its sale might bring several years of food, shelter and comfort to six poor lambs of God? And all said and done, Oiney concluded his passionate plea, the picture was returned intact without as much as a scratch on it. Surely all this deserved clemency?

During the latter part of his speech, Oiney wondered why the Bishop kept shaking his head and blowing air through his pursed lips. Finally the great man arose and paced up and down the richly carpeted floor. 'What a great, great pity,' he said sadly.

Oiney's eyes lit up with hope. 'So you are sorry for me friend, your Worship?'

'Not so much that, I'm afraid. The painting I'm talking about: it should never have been returned. Only one painting you say: what a pity!'

'So you are not angry, your Worship?'

'Angry? Good heavens, no! I'd be delighted if all the pictures and paintings in churches were to disappear from the face of the earth!'

'You would!' gasped the astonished Oiney.

'Yes, and all the statues and Stations of the Cross as well.' Oiney's gaping mouth opened wider and his eyes wore a startled look as the Bishop continued.

'I wouldn't bat an eyelid if they all were bundled over the Cliffs of Moher into the waves of the Atlantic or a huge bonfire made of them on the Hills of Slane.'

'Even . . . even the Blessed Virgin?' whispered Oiney in shuddering anticipation.

'The Blessed Virgin especially,' roared the Bishop now fully in flight with one of his pet themes. 'Ireland is thoroughly saturated with statue worship and mariolatry. I would like to sweep the lot into oblivion. Only that I cannot associate with criminals, I would like to shake your friend's hand.'

It was Oiney's turn to explode. 'You're not shakin' nobody's hand! Talkin' about the Blessed Virgin like she was Guy Fawkes!' Oiney made the sign of the Cross and thought hard and wildly. 'I'm writin' to the Pope,' he said threateningly. 'That's what I'm doin' – I'm writin' to the Pope.'

The Bishop of Meath stared intently at the young fellow shaking with anger in his seat. Then the truth dawning on him, he threw back his head and roared with hilarious laughter. 'Write to the Pope! Oh my God, it's rich, it's rich. Listen, sonny, I see, I see. You thought I was the Catholic Bishop of Meath. Oh, Lord above, how funny, how funny. You see, Mr what's-this-they-call-you . . . oh yes . . . Mr

Hoy, I'm the Protestant Bishop of Meath. How's that for a little faux-pas?' And again he burst into rollicking laughter. 'But we all make mistakes, laddie, even bishops. We will have tea together, shan't we? Christine,' he shouted going towards the door – but as soon as his back was turned, Oiney took a flying leap out through the bay window over the verandah and a mighty descent onto the lawn, a leap that easily matched the great feat of his spiritual ancestor in the Carrick Hills. He ran down the avenue from the Bishop's residence as though he was escaping from Hell itself, and ran breathlessly, pursued by two yapping poodles nipping his heels.

After this most embarrassing experience Oiney made full certain that he would present himself at the proper Bishop of Meath's house – well, the one that he thought proper. The Catholic Bishop was the antithesis of his jovial counterpart. He was tall, lean, sallow and ascetic. He seldom smiled and had deep, dark eyes which seemed to bore into Oiney's conscience, making him feel uncomfortable. After listening to his visitor's long, rambling, sad story, the Bishop raised his eyebrows and said, 'Oh, we shan't hang him. But tell me, young man, what do you think I can do?'

'Well, your Eminence, if you could say something favourable for Bobby it might help. I'm sure it would.'

'I never liked that particular painting,' said the Bishop. 'You didn't?'

'No, it was never my cup of tea, aesthetically I mean . . .'

'Aistwhat?' said Oiney

'Artistically. It was so sordid and sombre that I had it hidden above the Confessional. The obscure artist who painted it was a professional idiot. The rope around poor Judas's scrawny neck is not even taut and that thin branch to which it is tied could not even support a small sack of spuds.'

'That's right, your Holiness,' Oiney agreed, even though he had scarcely glanced at the painting. 'So you'll plead for clemency for poor Bobby, your Worship?'

'I will, surely. I will make such a speech that will put the great Demosthenes himself in the shade. Besides, we cannot allow three, or four is it, children of his to be crying out last thing at night for their fish suppers, can we?' The Bishop gave Oiney a very wan but knowing smile.

'Four of them, your Holiness,' said the astonished Oiney. 'But them's Bobby's exact words. How did you know?'

'Oh, Bobby Brown and I have had our dealings before. I'm afraid his interest in ecclesiastics is rather intense.'

The trial took place in Dundalk Court. Oiney's hopes were high until he saw the grim face of the notorious old Circuit Judge Ritchie on the bench. The arrival of the tall Bishop raised his spirits a little, even though that good man had to be helped into Court by two able assistants. After a disappointingly weak defence case, the prisoner threw himself at the mercy of the Court and admitted his guilt, giving Oiney at the same time one of those cute, twitching winks of his. The Bishop then rose to plead mitigation of sentence. He gave a heartrending description of the sorrow and onus which descends on the shoulders of the custodian of Church goods when something in his care is abused or stolen. Yet in the spirit of the good Jesus himself, he had left his sick bed to travel a fair distance to plead leniency for this seasoned sinner.

The Bishop continued in this poignant, plaintive manner and Oiney shuddered as he noticed several women and even some hardened businessmen on the jury take out their handkerchiefs and weep openly and profusely – not for the lost sheep, unfortunately, but the poor shepherd himself. The stony-faced Ritchie summed up everyone's sentiments. 'We must save our good Bishop from his own kindness. He has left his sick bed in his frail old age to come here and plead for a miserable hardened sinner and a cloister thief from Belfast. Are you not ashamed of yourself, Mr Brown, to not only witness but be the root cause of this man's sufferings? We must teach you a lesson, indeed.'

It was thus Bobby Brown got a much stiffer sentence on account of Oiney's effort. And now he earnestly wished that the good Bishop had stayed in his bed and died peacefully.

Ghost Story

A dispirited Oiney walked the streets of Dundalk that afternoon. His mission of mercy had failed miserably, his pockets
were empty and he had nowhere to shelter for the night.
He would have to find some stable or outhouse up one of
the entries off these busy little streets. He loitered at the
railway station for a while watching the train to Clones and
Creevan draw out, but still fearful of his granny's wrath, he
turned away from the platform and dandered slowly down
past the old churchyard and the monument over the grave
of the sister of the great poet, Robert Burns. He passed
the large hotel at the foot of the street to arrive at the
Maid of Erin statue. This is the rich legendary country of
Cuchulainn, Ireland's greatest folk hero; Oiney had read all
about him in that enchanting book *Celtic Romance*. From
here up to Carlingford and beyond to the slopes of the
Mourne mountains and the southern boundaries of Down
and Armagh lay the ancient plain of Muirtheme, the Gap
of the North, renowned in the colourful sagas of the Red
Branch knights and the warriors of Finn MacCool, the
Irish giant. Hungry though he was, Oiney felt elated by
their memory even, breathing as it were the same air and
walking in their footsteps.

It was on a public bench near the Maid of Erin statue
that he encountered the Creevan man Bert Corrigan. At
first Oiney hesitated, afraid that news of his whereabouts
might seep back to his irate granny, but his hunger and his
curiosity got the better of him and he approached the man.

'Is that yourself, Bert?'

Bert stared in amazement. 'Well, if it isn't Oiney!
Where in God's name have you been, Oiney? All Creevan's

talkin' about you an' mystified by your sudden disappearance. Some say that the Wee Folk snatched you for cutting down the Lone Tree; others tell the quarest stories about you hitch-hikin' to America in a Flyin' Fortress, but the strongest rumours are that you have a job dealin' with horses in the north of Dublin and have applied to join a Trappist monastery in north Tipperary.'

Oiney could not resist a good laugh. 'Just leave it to the Creevan folk, Bert, to get it all mixed up. How is me granny doin', Bert?'

'Fair to middlin', Oiney, but she's still rampagin'. She says she won't send you on a message again in a hurry. An' there was this big hulkin' brute from Dublin came pesterin' her about your whereabouts an' runnin' you down to the lowest. In the hinderend she paid Jemmy McGurk, Jonjo and another lad to pitch him into the deep end of Creevan lough.'

Oiney clapped his hands and gave a great hop of delight. 'Oh, good for her, Bert, good for her. O'Reilly himself would be no match for the Holy Terror.'

'You should watch the company you keep, Oiney. That big fella slunk out of Creevan with his tail between his legs, but he was swearin' revenge. He said he would get you if he had to search the sewers of Hell. If I was you, Oiney, I'd steer clear of yon fella.'

'What are you doin' in Dundalk, Bert?'

'I'm waitin' here on the single-decker bus to Blackrock. You'll hardly believe it, Oiney, but I bought a neat wee pub on this bit of headland at the near end of the village. It's called "Uncle Tom's Cabin". I read the book but the title's the best part of it. I was in Court this mornin', a smugglin' case. That Ritchie one, the judge, would hang a dog for trespassin'. Remember him on Creevan brae? I never laughed so much to see oul' frosty face with his bowler on an' biddin' the time o' day to the women . . .'

'Bert?'

'What is it, Oiney?'

'I don't want to go back to Creevan just yet.'

'Don't worry, Oiney! There's a spare room in my place if you want it. You're welcome, Oiney. Sure I knew your mother afore you were born. It was me that helped her, God rest her, with her Da's coffin to Castleblayney poorhouse. I watched you grow up with the Holy Terror an' Heaven knows she's not the aisiest woman in the world to live with. Everyone in Creevan knows that, but sure it takes all kinds ... Here's the bus comin', Oiney. Let's be off!' He put a friendly arm around Oiney's shoulder and led him to the bus stop.

At Blackrock the bus drew to a halt about fifty yards to the north of the Post Office and there on a grassy headland looking out both on sea and shore stood the cosy little tavern called 'Uncle Tom's Cabin'. It was a popular inn for both locals and visitors. Blackrock was a lively village with a long promenade and a colourful row of shops and hotels. Outside the shop doors there hung bright little sand buckets and spades, balloons and stick windmills. From a skating rink not far from the 'Cabin' a loudspeaker blared out popular tunes. Happy, smiling holidaymakers thronged the street and walked along the promenade with their children; some wore sunshades or dark glasses. Far away to the south one could see the faint cliff of Annagasson Point on the horizon, a mysterious beckoning wonder to a child, like the edge of the world. The long gentle ripple of the sands leading out of Dundalk Bay to meet the sea seemed endless, as though the waves were weary or else reluctant to reach the land.

Oiney had a room to himself at the inn; he helped to repay Bert's kindness by lifting tumblers, drying dishes and sweeping the floor. He would have felt perfect contentment in Blackrock, except for two nagging worries: his granny and that irate parasite, O'Reilly. Oiney was so proud of his granny's stand against the creature. She was an indomitable woman surely, and many a time walking along the quiet sands away from the crowded beach, he would think of long summers past, when she had held his hands and jumped up and down with him in these waves. Nothing pleased him better now than to sit in a quiet niche among the rounded rocks and gaze out at the wide immensity of the sea. There he would reflect on his terrible year of adventure in the wicked world. His sins he hoped were merely venial not mortal, but even they merited him a few thousand years in Purgatory, an uncomfortable region, he imagined, halfway between Hell and Heaven, where one lived on simple fare like bread and water and in perpetual twilight like his granny's coal-hole. He shuddered at the thought of it. The sooner he made his terrible confession the better. It brought him some solace to know that the Blackrock priest would be a complete stranger to him.

The chapel lay on the slight crest of a hill a little up from 'Uncle Tom's Cabin' and overlooking the bay. Oiney climbed the steps hoping to find the priest on call. A dark figure crossed the path at the top of the hill and went in through the main doorway, the priest or the sexton. Oiney was glad to find the chapel almost empty; an old woman was just finishing the Stations of the Cross and about to leave. In a side aisle, the curtain of the middle compartment of the Confession Box rustled and the anxious sinner gave a sigh of relief. The priest was on duty and soon the worst would be over; he would then enjoy that wonderful exaltation of a clear conscience and a cleansed soul. He went into the shadows of the box and waited until the small grille door was drawn aside.

'Father, forgive me for I have sinned.'

'How long, young man, since your last confession?'

'A year, Father.'

'A what?'

He heard the priest growl ominously. 'A year, Father.'

'Disgraceful. Carry on! Let us have them!'

'Father, you won't like this but I was involved in blowing up the Border.'

There was a dreadful hushed silence as though the good priest had dropped dead. 'Good God,' said the confessor, 'but carry on!'

'I masqueraded as a Cistercian monk, Father, an' I sold French Letters in the streets o' Dublin.'

'Merciful Jesus,' cried the priest, 'is there no end to your depravity?'

Oiney felt really sorry he had come but there was no way out of it now. 'I thought they were balloons, Father.'

'Stop adding lies to your iniquity!'

'I . . . I helped this Protestant steal a holy picture from Drogheda an' I didn't believe in Blessed Oliver's head.'

'Christ almighty,' roared the priest, 'aren't you the blackest, most accursed sinner ever to darken this box? Aren't you the dyed-in-the-wool scoundrel? Let me hear the rest of your behaviour!'

Oiney was glad that he had nothing else to confess. 'I've no more sins to confess, Father.'

'No more you say. Come off it you bloody little liar!' Oiney knelt, mouth wide open with astonishment at the vehemence and coarseness. He had been reprimanded in Confession before but this grilling made his own local priest, Father Duffy, seem like an angel. But he was in for a bigger shock.

A voice roared in his ears, 'Have I got to squeeze it out of you?' Then a great hairy hand shot around the corner of the box and grabbed him by the neck. 'So you've no more sins. What about the the vilest sin of all, tearin' apart the holy vows of matrimony between man an' wife an' dhrivin' me a ragin' beast through the provinces of Ireland to desthroy you, you little verminous insect?' The coarse voice and the hairy hand of O'Reilly were now too obvious to Oiney; the bully was raging mad as he dragged his young enemy out into the deserted aisle which re-echoed with his insane laughter. The grip tightened on Oiney's throat but when he saw O'Reilly dressed in a black suit like a priest his own fury mounted at this desecration of holiness and now with the little breath left in him he managed to gasp, 'Are you not ashamed of yourself, Mr O'Reilly, doin' the very same as that dirty Yeoman captain in the Croppy days, disguisin' yourself as a man o' the cloth in Confession to vent your anger on me? God or man'll never forgive you!'

The taunt only served to make the brute more angry. 'Who are you to talk about disguises you pious little prig,' he shouted, tightening his squeeze until the veins stood out on his victim's temples. 'You that masqueraded not only as a monk but a very saint . . .'

Stars flashed through poor Oiney's brain as he bravely muttered a last Act of Contrition for his invisible soul when suddenly the greatest miracle of his young life happened.

A slow, ponderous bell rang out in the chapel belfry and resounded over Blackrock. The hand suddenly relaxed its hold on Oiney's throat and joined another hairy hand in pious supplication. It was none other than the Angelus bell struck each day at noon. Ever since he was a child, O'Reilly had been taught to relinquish every other activity, no matter how important, at the very first peal of this bell. Even through critical moments in long years of service as a garda, the habit had become so engrained that it was really second nature to him. Oiney, of course, blessed himself as well, but more in gratitude than real piety. And then in a flash he took to his heels and ran out of the chapel into the sunlight and down the path to the safety of 'Uncle Tom's Cabin'. Even as he ran, he thanked God for the staunch devotion of the Irish people.

Bert Corrigan's face wore a look of deep concern as the breathless Oiney almost collapsed into a chair in the bar. When he had recovered a little he told his friend how he had encountered his enemy in the Confessional.

'He'll come to a bad end that scoundrel,' said Bert angrily. 'But I'm afraid there's even worse news, Oiney. This telegram arrived an hour ago from Creevan for you.' Though his heart fluttered and his fingers shook, Oiney opened the envelope:

YOUR GRANDMOTHER DIED THIS MORNING STOP
COME HOME FOR THE FUNERAL STOP
SIGNED FATHER DUFFY PARISH PRIEST STOP

The two men looked at each other in sad silence.

An hour later Oiney sat in the carriage of the train on the way home to Creevan. Bert had provided him with some money to cover funeral expenses, but he dearly wished that he had not to return to the wee town in such solemn reverie. He still felt a sense of guilt towards his granny. Admittedly she too had her faults, but God knows, she had her good points. She had bought him that green gansey and all his other clothes and given him holidays at the seaside as a boy. Many of her strange doings made him smile. Those dreadful prayers she used to say at the doorstep as the pious passed on the way to chapel. And her corns and bunions on Lough Derg. It was hard to believe he would see her no more. He would love to have told her the least harmful of his adventures but perhaps in the Kingdom above she was reading the unabridged edition of his every deed. That Holy Terror of a granny, wherever could he hope to find her like again?

He felt very sad as the train moved under the shadow of the familiar Slieve Gullion and into the homeland of Paddy Kavanagh the poet and the great Gaelic bard of the nineteenth century, Art McCooey, close by Glasdrummond and Culloville. This was the western edge of the plain of Muirtheme and the Gap of the North. Soon they halted for a moment at Castleblayney station with its poorhouse walls still visible from the train. There it was that the two coffins had been brought that strange night of his grandfather's funeral among these little hills. What had made his granny the fierce indomitable woman she was? Perhaps the frightening tales of the terrible Famine she had heard as a child in the Carrick Hills when the memory of them was so fresh and bitter.

The train moved slowly into Creevan and he had a great view of the Bluebell Hill in full bloom above the lovely calm lough. A thrill of excitement ran through his veins, despite his sadness, to see his native fields and surrounds again. As the train drew to a halt, he looked out on the platform. My God, he thought, what am I seeing? He could not believe his eyes. Nor was it her ghost but her wee sturdy plump self, standing with the little brown jug in one hand while with a smile on her face she shook the other gnarled fist of welcome at Oiney. On either side of her stood those grinning pair of rogues, Jemmy McGurk and Jonjo, who had joined her conspiracy to send the fake telegram to lure him back to Creevan. Who in the world but herself would connive such a plan? And Creevan itself wasn't it splendid that day, none but a fool would leave it with its loughs and rivers and lush green fields and winding blackberry lanes in the hidden hills of Monaghan! Overhead on the tapering chapel spire above Jonjo's belfry the famous weathercock still had pride of place and Oiney smiled too remembering the tale and many others of his home in these little Ulster hills, tales that will endure in a world of peace, still to be won, aye, even a million years ere Ireland dreams of sinking in the wild Atlantic.

THE END